With Wings
as Eagles

With Wings as Eagles

Patsy Baker O'Leary

Houghton Mifflin Company
Boston   1997

*This is a work of fiction, a product of the author's
imagination. Any resemblance to actual events or persons,
living or dead, is entirely coincidental.*

For information about this and other Houghton Mifflin
trade and reference books and multimedia products, visit
The Bookstore at Houghton Mifflin on the World
Wide Web at http://www.hmco.com/trade/.

The text of this book is set in 13 pt. Bodoni Book.

Library of Congress Cataloging-in-Publication Data
O'Leary, Patsy Baker.
With wings as eagles / by Patsy Baker O'Leary.
p. cm.
Summary: In 1938 in rural North Carolina, twelve-year-old Bubba
Harkins finds himself in emotional turmoil when his father
returns from prison to resume his life with his wife and sons
and his black neighbors.
ISBN 0-395-70557-6
[1. Fathers and sons — Fiction. 2. Family life — Fiction.
3. Race relations — Fiction. 4. North Carolina — Fiction.] I. Title.
PZ7.046254Ch 1997
[Fic] — dc20 95-1666 CIP AC

Manufactured in the United States of America
BP 10 9 8 7 6 5 4 3 2 1

For
Shirley Rousseau Murphy
and
my father, Alton P. Baker,
and all the others
who believed

ACKNOWLEDGMENTS

There is no beginning or end to the list of those who helped in the creation of this novel: it would stretch from this land of my birth to my family and beyond. More immediately, my deep appreciation goes to Shirley Rousseau Murphy for her vision and support; Taylor Koonce, Harry Jarvis, and Jerry Raynor for their expertise; Frank Quinn, Gene Tyndall, and Ida Wooten Tripp, who remembered it the way it was; Thora Brothers, and my aunts, Marie O'Neal, Amy Hopkins, and Espie Wrenn, for helping me render the time and place true; my brother, Gene Baker, for some of his "adventures"; Paul Davenport, Sam Underwood, Herman Gus Moeller, James Langley, and Ralph Tyson for their "legal memories"; and Carl Goerch, Jerry Bledsoe, Roy Taylor, and others for their nostalgic writings. Words are inadequate to thank Barrie Van Dyck, my agent, for her faith and persistence; Norma Jean Sawicki for acquiring the book; and Anita Silvey and her staff at Houghton Mifflin for their skill and enthusiasm in shepherding it to publication.

In a sense, this book is not mine alone, for a special note of gratitude must go to all those who so generously shared their lives and memories to be woven into the fabric of *With Wings as Eagles* by the Source who tells all stories.

AUTHOR'S NOTE

Language changes, as do times and places. In the period and setting of *With Wings as Eagles*, it was customary to call African Americans "colored people," and in order to maintain authenticity, that is the term I have used. Southern speech patterns are a rich and varied language based on many heritages, and in trying to capture the eastern North Carolina dialect, I have also used colloquialisms, idioms, and certain spellings in the vernacular, such as *wont* for *was not*, *won't* for *will not*, and *holp* for *help*. Some of these date back to our country's early settlers, and many are still in use today.

1

The year was 1938, and soon the world would change and a time and way of life would be lost. But on this long-awaited day, one boy's world was changing, and he had no way of knowing the turn of its axis would take it into shadow.

Bubba Harkins strained to see any flicker of movement in the distance, but the hard-packed clay road glared empty in the heat, and in the weedy ditches, cattails stood like brown pokers dull with dust. His eyes smarted in the early morning sun.

"Bubba, you reckon he's really comin'?"

He glanced down at his little brother. "Sure he is, Scooter. Didn't Mama say so just this mornin'?" He looked back to the road, the businesslike air in his blue eyes more that of a man than of a twelve-year-old boy. Scooter was only five, but imitating

Bubba, he, too, squinted, his towhead shining in the sun.

The two boys sat on a small hill among the tilted markers of the family graveyard. On one side, the parallel tracks of their lane led to the homeplace and were lost in the shade of the chinaberry tree. The unpainted house, its kitchen connected by a breeze-way, stood silvered with time, the rusting tin and shake roof rich against the green of the umbrella-shaped tree. The still morning air felt heavy with the coming warmth of the day, but a wandering breeze inspired a bobwhite's call. A large dog lay between the boys, its black coat glistening in the sunlight.

"Bubba? Will he know us?"

"Why, sure, he's gone know us," Bubba answered. "We're his boys, ain't we?"

Scooter looked uncertain. "Well, he might know you, and Queen." The dog's eyes opened. "But he's never even seen me. How's he gone know me?"

Bubba gave him a shove. "Aw, come on. Didn't Mama send your picture to him, special? And didn't he write back and say you were a chip off the old block?"

Scooter brightened. "Hey, yeah, he sure did." They scanned the road again. "You see anything?"

"Not yet. Be a while, I 'spect," Bubba said. "It's a long way from Richmond to North Carolina." I ought to be more excited, he thought. He'd longed for the day his daddy would come home. But now dread lay like a stone in the anticipation that bubbled inside. He had just about worshiped his daddy, but the last six years and the nights hearing his mama cry as he huddled in his bed lay between then and now.

A crystalline green dragonfly hovered, then darted away as Scooter shifted his skinny rear on the ground.

"You better quit that squirming. You get grass stains on your clean pants, and Mama'll tan your hide."

"Well, I don't know why we had to get dressed up so early for, if he wont gone be here for a while."

" 'Cause she wants everything just right when he does get here. Now you hush your fussin' and behave."

"Fussin'? It ain't me been doing the fussin' this mornin'! Mama cleanin' and cookin' and makin' me put on my Sunday clothes, and it only Friday!"

"Well, she ain't gone calm down till he gets here."

"And you ain't been no better. Got that dog so brushed and clean, I reckon Daddy won't even know her."

"He'll know her. Queen was his dog."

"Wish he'd hurry," Scooter said. "I gotta pee."

"Then go behind them blackberry bushes." Bubba sighed as the boy ran off. He sure got tired sometimes looking after Scoot. With all he had to do, it would have been a big help if his brother had been older. At least Scooter would be starting school this year, and now Daddy'd be home to help.

He scanned the road again. Behind the cattails, the puffed gold heads of the devil's walking sticks leaned heavy in the heat. He thought of Ole Raggey's stick at school, and shivered.

A cloud of dust traveled toward them, and the knot of fear shifted like a live thing. Queen raised her head. "Hurry, Scooter. Somethin's coming!"

The boy ran out of the bushes, struggling with his pants buttons. "Where?"

Bubba pointed, and they watched as the dust swell neared. "Aw, shoot," Bubba said. It was just Mrs. Fields showing off her new black 1939 Lincoln again. The week before, Grady Ferrell had written a bad word in the dust down the passenger side, and she'd driven off leaving half the townsfolk laughing. Trouble was Grady's middle name.

She spotted them on the hill and waved, shaking her head as she sped by. The boys watched as the dust settled, then sat again.

"Bubba, what'd Mrs. Fields shake her head for?"

"I don't know."

"Seems like everybody does that lately, shake their heads when they see us."

"Aw, you just imaginin' things." But he'd seen it, too. The worry tightened his stomach again.

"Naw, I'm not. Just last Sunday, she gave me a nickel before church and nearly shook her head off, callin' me 'poor boy.' Why you reckon she said that?"

Bubba looked away. Likely 'cause folks knew their daddy was coming home, but his mama didn't want Scooter to know he'd been in prison, at least not till the boy was old enough to understand he was really innocent. Better tell him soon, though — he was starting to notice things, and Bubba was running out of answers.

"Bubba," Scooter began again, "why you reckon . . ."

"I heard you." God bless America, that boy was just like a dog with a bone, worrying somethin' to death. He hedged, "Reckon 'cause we are poor. Leastways, some folks think we are."

"Maybe that's how come she gave me the nickel," Scooter nodded wisely. "Is poor a bad thing to be?"

"Guess so, if you want to be rich."

The boy pushed at the ground with a stick. "You reckon he's gone like us?"

"Sure."

"How you know?"

Bubba gave it thought. " 'Cause he has to, that's why. He's our daddy. He has to like us."

"Why does he have to, just 'cause he's our daddy?"

"Just because, that's why. Now hush — I can't watch the road and listen to your jabber, too."

Scooter looked startled at his tone and saw Bubba tearing at a blade of grass. The boy took a deep breath. "Bubba . . . I'm scared."

"Ain't nothin' to be scared of."

"Then how come you tearing that grass to bits?"

Surprised, Bubba looked at the shreds of grass on his sweaty palms. He scowled at Scooter's satisfied smile and brushed his hands on his pants.

He couldn't help it, things just didn't feel right. Even last night when Israel and his wife Lily had come over, the man wasn't himself. He'd stayed quiet, his eyes distant, his brown-skinned hands with their yellowed nails working his old gray felt hat in circles. Israel and his daddy had been friends from way back.

"Bubba! Look!"

A new billow of dust rose on the horizon. Bubba's armpits prickled. As he stood, Queen came up beside him. The cloud moved nearer, and the engine's hum grew louder until it vibrated the stone in Bubba's chest. He licked a drop of sweat off his lip.

The lumbering bus slowed, an eddy of dust fanning out behind. It passed them and stopped. A man carrying a small suitcase got out and then was obscured by the powdery haze as the bus rattled away.

Bubba watched the solitary figure walk toward their house. He saw his mother's bright red dress as she came on the porch and heard the faint slap of the screen door closing behind her. She lifted her hand to shade her eyes. The summer quiet hung again in the air, until a mourning dove's call drifted from the chinaberry tree as the man stopped to shift his case. Then straightening his back, he walked on again.

Scooter whooped, shattering the spell, and ran down the hill. At the grove of pecan trees, he looked back, calling, "Hey, Bubba, come on! Daddy's home!"

Bubba paused, then loped after him, Queen following with a joyful yelp.

Through the trees, he saw his mother run off the porch with a cry. As she came into the sunlight, her red dress held the light, then blurred as she dashed to the man. His arms went around her, bunching his loose gray suit around his neck. Her cry of "Jed" and his soft "Ruby" made the boys stop.

"Bubba?" Scooter whispered. "Mama's cryin'."

"That's 'cause she's happy."

They waited, Bubba with a quiet dignity, Scooter suddenly shy. The dog growled low in her chest.

"Hush, Queen," Bubba murmured.

"Yeah, Queen, can't you tell that ain't no stranger?" Scooter echoed.

Their mother spotted them and with a proud gesture pointed them out to the man. A slow smile lit his thin face as he held out his arms. "Bubba? Scooter?" When they still hesitated, his arms dropped. "Ain't you gone welcome your daddy home?"

Scooter looked at Bubba, uncertain, and then he took off running, his feet leaving puffs of dust behind. With a leap, he was in the man's arms. Jed pulled back to look at him. "That's got to be Scooter, all right," he said, and the boy laughed as he was swung in the air.

Bubba's heart hammered as he anchored his feet in the floury dust. He wanted with all his heart to be young again like Scooter and run to his daddy's arms, but something held him back. His father didn't seem as big as he remembered and even had a bald patch on his head. Bubba looked at his mama's tears, and the heavy stone moved again in his chest. It seemed a stranger had come; this wasn't the daddy he remembered — the man who was going to stop his mother's tears, who would make everything all right and be in charge again. Why, his daddy had been twice that big, with broad shoulders and muscles that bulged from the hard labor of the farm. How could he give back the job of being the man of the house to this skinny stranger?

Putting Scooter down, the man turned to look at him. "Bubba? Is that really Bubba?" Ruby nodded. Bubba steeled himself and defiantly looked back — at the same clear eyes that he remembered, with their blue faded from working in the glaring sun. Something moved painfully inside him. He saw the tears rise in his father's eyes, and felt an answering sting in his own.

The man opened his arms. "You too big to give your daddy a hug? Or are you still my boy?" he asked.

Bubba hesitated, his heart pounding. His throat was closed so tight he couldn't speak. He looked at his mama. She nodded, her smile not quite straight, a glance of light catching the shimmer in her eyes.

He pushed against the resistance holding him back and stepped forward. The man engulfed him in a hug, not seeming to notice that Bubba had only slid one arm around him in a halfhearted gesture of greeting.

2

Bubba picked up a piece of firewood, not really seeing it. His daddy's return that day had made things different already. In the kitchen his mother was humming "What a Friend We Have in Jesus," here was Scooter dancing impatiently for more wood, and even the weathered homeplace had a glow from the late afternoon sun. But he still couldn't shake his sense of unease.

"Hurry up, Bubba!"

"I'm hurryin'." He loaded two more pieces of kindling on the pile in the boy's arms. "That's all you can tote. Won't do you much good to show off in front of Daddy if you spill it all."

Staggering, Scooter stepped up on the breezeway connecting the detached kitchen to the house. He glanced down the porch, then went on inside.

With a sigh, Bubba loaded his own arms and followed. Queen lay on the cool dirt under the floor of the breezeway and thumped her tail as he stepped up. A bird's cry came from close by, and he saw a mockingbird take flight, the white band on its wings flashing as

9

it lifted from the grass to the branches of the tree. A voice startled him. "Pretty sight, ain't it?"

The man was sitting in his daddy's rocker, the evening breeze curling the blue smoke from his corncob pipe. The smell reminded Bubba of many a long-gone evening when his daddy had sat in just that way after washing up for supper, and a longing swept him. But this man's shirt and overalls hung loose. The square hand holding the pipe was soft, and the veins under the white skin stood out like twisting cords. Bubba had been surprised at how little his back was when he'd put his arm around him. And later when he'd washed up, Bubba had seen dirty-looking scars on his back. He'd looked away, queasy at the roil in his stomach. He went on into the kitchen, letting the screen door slap behind him. His daddy sure had changed.

"Boy, you took your sweet time," taunted Scooter as he came in. "I coulda had three loads in here by now."

"I hear you talking, but I don't see no three loads," said Bubba.

"You boys hush that bickerin'. This is a happy day for us, and I got no time for such mess," their mama said. She turned the sizzling pieces of chicken in the fry pan, her face flushed from the room's heat. A bib apron covered the front of her red dress, and strands of her blond hair curled against her moist cheek. As Bubba unloaded his wood into the box behind the stove, he noticed she looked younger than he could remember in a long time. The worry lines had eased out, and her eyes were full of light. The grease popped, and she jumped back, bumping into Scooter. "I swan, what you doing right under my feet? Go visit with your daddy. Too hot in here anyway." Scooter ran outside. "You too, Bubba."

"Reckon I'd just as soon stay and help, Mama." He stopped, worried. "He won't say nothin' to Scooter, will he?" A shadow flickered in her eyes, but she shook her head.

He was unloading firewood into the box behind the kitchen stove when Scooter came back in, excited because his daddy had said they could go swimming in the creek and was there time before dinner?

"What you mean, go swimmin'? I ain't got no time to take you swimmin' right now," Bubba said.

"You don't have to. Daddy's going."

"Well, if that ain't just like your daddy!"

"Then can we go, Mama? Please?"

"All right, but you all don't stay long. I ain't cookin' this special dinner for waitin'," she said as she patted out biscuits.

"Come on, Bubba — he says for you to come, too."

"You go on. I'll help Mama." Bubba avoided his mother's eyes and watched through the screen door as Scooter ran up to join his daddy. As they walked off, he suddenly felt guilty about staying back. Most likely Scooter would do something foolish without him there.

Metal scraped against metal as Ruby slid the pan of

biscuits in the oven. "Whew!" she said, wiping her forehead. "You should have gone, water would have felt good. You gettin' too big to go swimmin', you growin' up faster than I thought."

"I'm twelve, Mama."

She laid her hand along his cheek. "An old twelve at that. You've had too much on you these last years."

Bubba blinked. He and his mama didn't exchange many soft words. It almost undid him now. Her eyes followed him as he shoved a stick of wood into the stove. The heat from the open burner made him quickly drop the damper lid back in place.

"Ain't you glad he's home?" Ruby asked.

"Sure I'm glad."

"You don't act like it. You ain't had two words to say all day. I thought you'd be all over yourself."

"I am glad, Mama. Really I am. It's just that . . ." She waited quietly, and he blurted it out, "He don't seem the same Daddy I remembered."

She smiled, relieved. "I reckon not. Six years is a long time. And him so skinny! Just you wait till I put some meat back on them bones. Things will be different, now he's home. Sometimes I didn't think this day would ever come." She glanced at the mirror on the wall. "Oh my mercy, I look a sight!" She smoothed back her hair and dabbed at her face with a cloth. When she started fanning herself with the apron, Bubba laughed. "Don't you laugh at me, boy! If that table's set, you go on outside. I'll put them biscuits on the warming shelf in a minute, and we'll go pull them boys out of that creek."

The reminder wiped away Bubba's smile as he went out the door. The leaves of the chinaberry tree stirred in the breeze, seeming to whisper Scooter's name. Bubba slapped absently at a mosquito. A worry danced at him, and he was relieved when he heard the oven door slam and saw his mama hang her apron on the nail by the door. Stepping out, she said, "My, that air feels good. That kitchen's hot enough to singe the feathers off a bird." Queen came from under the breezeway and followed them, her tail flagging. Bubba wanted to hurry on, but Ruby reached for his hand. "Son, don't look so sour. This is our happy day come at last. We ought to stop and praise the Lord right in this here path!"

"I know, Mama."

She glanced down and stopped. "Bubba, you never put on your shoes today!"

He looked at his dusty feet. "I forgot." He didn't want her to know his shoes were too small.

"Hmph. And I bet Scooter 'forgot,' too. And here I wanted you all to look special nice for your daddy."

"We did, Mama. I doubt he even noticed our feet."

She squeezed his hand as they went on. This was usually Bubba's favorite time of day, when the trees cast long shadows across the field, but now the green shade of the woods seemed threatening, and the breeze stirred the dusty leaves to a dry rustle. He

13

listened for sounds ahead, but a chattering flock of grackles settled in the trees. Finally he heard Scooter's high giggle and his daddy's laugh, and he breathed easier.

As they came out of the woods, the creek stretched out before them. The setting sun glinted gold off the water, blinding him. "There they are," Ruby pointed.

He stopped where he stood. Scooter was swimming too near the drop-off. He started to call a warning, then bit back the words. His daddy wouldn't appreciate him bossing his brother around when he was right there. Tense, he willed the boy to look at him.

He did, and shouted, "Look at me, Bubba!" as he scrambled onto a fallen tree and jumped, hitting the water in a crook-sided fall. Bubba stepped forward, but then Scooter came back up, throwing a glittering spray into the air. Jed waved to Ruby and didn't see the boy when he went down and at first didn't come up. When Scooter did surface, his arms were flailing and a frightened cry tore from his throat. "Bubba!"

"Oh sweet Jesus!" screamed Ruby.

Bubba ran and without breaking stride, dived. Just before he hit the water, he heard Jed cry out, "My God, my God — the drop-off!" then the water streaked cold fingers through his hair, and the green silence of the underwater enveloped him. Surfacing for air, he saw Jed swimming toward them and dived again. In the murky water, he saw a glimmer of movement. A submerged stob scraped his leg, and then Scooter came clear, thrashing in panic, his fingernails raking across Bubba's arm. He was hard to hold, a ferment of arms and legs, elbows and knees. Suddenly he went limp. Lungs aching, Bubba gripped his hair and kicked, sending them both up from the cool depths to the warm surface water. Gasping, he got his arm around Scooter's neck. Jed reached for the boy, but Bubba ignored him and headed for shore. He saw Queen paddling toward him and turn to follow as he passed.

His heart drumming, Bubba laid the unconscious boy facedown and started pressing his back. Queen nosed up beside him with a soft whine.

"Here, let me do that, son," Jed gasped as Ruby hurried up to them.

"You get away! He's my brother and I'll take care of him!" Bubba slapped his father's hands away. "Don't you touch him!" Queen growled, and Jed stepped back.

"Bubba!" his mama cried.

Jed put a hand on her arm. "It's all right, Ruby. Let him do it — looks like he knows how. When he gets tired, I can help."

Bubba pressed again, then looked at the man with hard eyes. All the confused emotions he had felt this day narrowed down to this moment. "You helped enough already." He leaned his weight on Scooter's back again. "What'd you let him play down there for, anyway? You knew that hole was there — you told me bout it enough times yourself."

Jed looked at Ruby, his hands spread. "I don't know how I came to forget it, and that's the truth."

With a "Huh!" under his breath, Bubba pressed and released again and again, his thoughts following the rhythm of his hands. Forgot. Huh. Forgot that hole. The slack muscles in the small back tightened as Scooter coughed and vomited up the creek water. Bubba turned him over. The boy was still unconscious as he lifted him in his arms.

Jed stepped forward. "Give him to me. He's too heavy for you."

"No, he's not," Bubba said, defiant. "I been taking care of him all his life, and I can carry him."

"Now Bubba, this has gone far enough," Jed said. "You ain't strong enough to carry him all the way back to the house. Give him here. I can take care of him."

"Like you took care of him while he was swimmin'?" He avoided his father's stricken eyes, seeing only the stranger that had intruded himself into their world that day. "You ain't fit to take care of nobody!"

He saw his mama's hands held out as if to ward off hurt to the man. Bubba's resentment tasted bitter as he shifted his brother's weight in his arms and started home, Queen at his heels.

The gloom of the woods raised goose pimples on his wet skin as he left the sunlight. His clothes clung in damp patches, and Scooter's body was the only spot of warmth he felt. He tried to keep his back straight, for he felt his mama's worried eyes and knew Jed was right behind and watching, too.

Huh. That man acted like he could just walk in and take over like he'd never been away. But a lot had happened between then and now. Bubba hadn't forgotten how his mama had looked that day when she came back from town without his daddy, with her eyes lost and her stomach swelling out before her like a weight. And that night Scooter had come, and he'd had to help Lily with the birthing. From that day on, he'd had to be a man.

Scooter's weight strained against his arms, and he remembered how Lily had handed his brother to him that long-ago night — just a little thing, didn't weigh no more than nothing, it seemed. And feel him now!

He pulled more air into his lungs. His real daddy wouldn't have let Scooter swim at that part of the creek, nor forgot that hole, nor let Bubba slap his hands off. He wouldn't have put up with such mess. This man had just stood there and took it. For the first time, Bubba wondered if his father had deserved to go to jail. He would've sworn his daddy wouldn't have no truck with moonshinin', but maybe he'd been wrong.

Scooter's eyes were still shut, his lashes spiky against his pale skin, and a bruise was rising on his forehead. My lordamercy, a ripple of fear crossed Bubba's mind, you reckon he's gone be all right? He quickened his steps, almost stumbling on the uneven ground. The walk back had never seemed so long. By the time he saw his mama run past to get things ready, his muscles were quivering and the sight of home had never been so sweet.

The screen slapped as Ruby went in, then Jed was on the porch, holding the door open. Bubba carried Scooter in sideways, leaving a wet trail on the rose-patterned linoleum in the sitting room. In the shadowed bedroom, his mama waited with the bedcovers turned back. Heart pounding, he laid Scooter on the straw tick mattress, and as Ruby started toweling him, he said, "He ain't opened his eyes yet, Mama."

"He ain't?" she looked up, startled.

"No ma'am. He's got a goose egg. Must've hit himself bad."

She pushed back Scooter's wet hair. "Better get me some ice and bring it here. Hurry now."

He turned to go, and saw his father standing in the doorway. Bubba had forgotten all about him for a minute. After all, he and his mama were used to taking care of things by themselves.

Jed stepped aside as he came through the door. Hurrying onto the porch, Bubba heard him say in a low voice, "Ruby, anything I can do?"

"I don't know," she answered. "If he don't come around soon, you might have to go fetch the doctor."

Go fetch Doc Swinson? They never did that unless they had to. Bubba didn't wait to hear any more. Lord, let Scooter be all right, he prayed as he jerked open the kitchen door. The wall of heat felt good to his cold skin. Grabbing a flour-sack towel and pick, he jabbed at the half-melted block of ice in the icebox on the kitchen porch.

Returning with the cold bundle in his hands, he found Jed still standing in the doorway and his mama beside the bed, like statues, waiting. The dust motes drifting in the ray of sunlight from the window were the only movement in the room. Scooter was lying straight out, his damp hair curled against the pillow. First time I've seen him laying like that, Bubba thought. Usually he's sprawled out all over the bed, his half and my half, too, or curled up like a scared caterpillar. He didn't look natural. More like he was . . . The fear walked up his neck again.

3

His mama reached for the ice, and he was relieved to see someone move. The sunbeam slanting from the window caught in her hair as she lay the ice against the bruise. She looked up. Surprised, he saw she was looking past him at Jed, her mute appeal sharp as a cry.

"I'll go get the doctor," Jed said. "Israel still got that

truck?" She nodded. He stopped Bubba's move to the door. "You stay and help your mama."

"But . . ."

"No buts. Do what I say, boy!" Jed snapped. Then his blue eyes softened, "Best way you can help Scooter right now, son." And he was gone.

Through the window, Bubba watched him sprint across the yard and hung to the knowledge that they could trust Israel to get help. He and Lily loved Scoot like he was their own, even if he wasn't colored.

"Bubba, bring me some of that hot water off the stove. His skin is still just like ice."

This time the kitchen's heavy smell of fried chicken made spit flood his mouth, and he barely made it out the back door in time to throw up. The bile stung his nose, and a cold sweat popped out on his forehead. Wiping his face with his damp sleeve, he leaned against the cistern, grateful for the sun-soaked warmth of the stone. Queen nuzzled him with a soft cry.

"Bubba, you comin' with that water?"

"Yes'm." He hurried back in the kitchen and splashed cold water from the pump on his face. Holding his breath, he ladled hot water from the stove reservoir into a tin molasses bucket, grateful for the cut of the wire handle in his hand, for it took his mind off the sight of the blueberry pie his mama had fixed for their big homecoming dinner.

As he came out of the kitchen, he saw a dust cloud

rising down the road, and he let out a slow breath. Back in the bedroom, he felt his mama's eyes as he poured the water into the washstand bowl. He avoided looking at Scooter, for fear his stomach would bolt again.

"You're right white. You been sick?"

"I'm all right now."

"You sure?" He nodded. "Then hold this ice while I wash him down." She dipped a cloth in the hot water. "Sure hope your daddy and Israel get back soon."

"Saw the truck leaving. Israel will hurry." At her look, he added quickly, "I mean, they might have to chase all over to find Doc Swinson."

"My land, I hope not." Wringing out the cloth, she asked, "Bubba, whatever got into you today? You know better than to talk to your daddy like that."

"He's not my daddy."

She stopped, her eyes wide, "What you mean? Of course he's your daddy!"

"No, he ain't. He don't look like my daddy, and he don't act like my daddy. Even Queen don't know him."

"I never heard such. Reckon I ought to know who he is better than some dog." She snapped the cloth open and rubbed it over Scooter's arms and legs until his skin flushed pink, then covered him. "All right, I'll hold that ice for a while now. You get some air."

He knew she wanted to be alone to pray. He had heard her many a night, talking to God like he was her best friend, but seemed to him a friend wouldn't let happen all the bad things that had happened to his mama.

He sat on the porch steps to wait. The sun was about set now, no longer casting shadows, just a light haze across the land. Off in the yard a cricket sang, and through the silhouetted branches of the chinaberry tree, he saw one star in the deepening blue of the sky.

Queen's nails clicked on the floorboards, and she slumped against him with a sigh. He rubbed the loose skin on her neck as he listened for the truck returning, but all he heard were the cricket and the whisper of his mother's prayers through the open bedroom window.

They should have been back by now. Bubba's eyes strained against the dark for any sign of headlights, but he only saw more stars scattered in the dim shape of the tree. He shifted on the hard wooden steps. A square of golden light spilled from the bedroom window. His mama had lit the kerosene lamp long ago.

Reckon they're having a hard time gettin' up with Doc Swinson, he thought. He knew he should have gone with them. He didn't care what his mama said — that man couldn't take care of things. He'd bout killed Scooter already.

He swallowed down his fear.

The clock chimed, and he heard his mama moving

inside as she lit the sitting room lamp. She came to the door, "Any sign?"

He shook his head no, and she sighed as she went back inside. Then Queen sat up, her ears perked at the same time he heard the motor. Headlight beams swung in an arc as the truck turned into the lane. Ruby came back to the door, and he saw her shadow lying long in the light on the porch as they waited.

Only two people got out of the truck — his father and Israel, whose white shirt and faded overalls stood out against his dark skin and the night. Surprised, Bubba noticed how he loomed over Jed. He'd always thought they were of a size.

The men stepped onto the porch, Queen thumping her tail as Israel patted her head. Jed opened the door and nodded for Israel to step inside. The big man hesitated, then scraped his shoes clean on the floorboards, pulled off his hat, and went in.

Bubba heard them tell his mama the doctor would be coming after he made another call, that they'd had to wait while he finished his supper. Through the screen, Bubba saw her disbelieving look. "Finished his supper? Didn't you tell him our boy was knocked out cold?"

"We told him, Miss Ruby," Israel said.

"He said boys got knocked in the head all the time, and we owed him money, and he wont gone be at the beck and call of some jailbird," Jed added.

She looked at Israel. "He said that?" He nodded, his eyes down. "But he *is* coming?"

"In his own good time," Jed said, bitter. "Acted like he was doing us a favor."

Israel looked at Jed. "It wont that bad."

"It wont good, neither. I doubt he would have come at all, if you hadn't been there. Didn't want to shame a white man in front of a colored, I reckon."

Bubba felt sick. Now his brother might die because his daddy was treated like white trash. Been better if I'd gone myself, he thought. Everybody knows I pay what I owe, even if it's a nickel at a time. Ole Doc Swinson and his 'money owed'! We don't owe him but fifty cents right now, down from the five dollars he charged when Mama was sick with pneumonia last year.

Ruby sighed. "Well, nothin' to do but wait, then."

"You want I should go get Lily to sit with you?"

"I'd take that right kindly, Israel."

Israel came out the door and saw him. "Hey there, Bubba. You want to ride with me?"

Bubba nodded and climbed into the truck, breathing in deep the pungent smells of old leather, cured tobacco, and summer sweat. The truck jerked as Israel slammed it into gear, and Bubba rolled down the window to let the breeze hit his face. The house looked small against the night, the chinaberry tree blending in so it looked all of a piece. They rocked down the lane to the main road, then speeded up. The

24

headlights caught in the bushes by the roadside, making them pass like ghosts.

Israel hummed under his breath as he drove, the dim light from the dashboard glinting off his cheeks and nose and catching an occasional sparkle from his eyes as they scanned the road. Bubba liked Israel's face, solid and square-built, with the curliest eyelashes he'd ever seen, and even in the dark he knew the brown eyes were steady and kind. He reckoned he'd learned at least a thousand things from that man. Israel's hands had a wisdom of their own — they knew how to fix things, make things grow, gentle an animal. There was life in his hands. "Israel? You think Scooter's gone be all right?"

Israel glanced at him. "I 'magine so. Surprises me most kids ever do grow up, they hurt themselves so much and all." He blinked and didn't say any more, and Bubba knew Benjamin was on his mind. Israel still grieved for his dead son, and now here was Scooter bad hurt and might die. For the first time he understood what Israel felt. The truck's tires rumbled over the creek bridge, then Israel went on, "He gone be all right. The Lord ain't gone let nothin' happen to Scooter."

Bubba felt better. The memory of Israel's restless hands the night before came back, and he pushed himself farther up in the seat. "Israel, does my daddy seem the same to you?"

"Reckon so. Little bit skinnier, little bit whiter." He

laughed his deep throaty laugh. "Round here, that might be a good thing."

"He ain't the same to me."

"Suppose not. Somepin' like what your daddy been through leave a mark, inside and out. Matter of fact, you both done changed these six years. He's prob'ly wonderin' what happened to that little boy Bubba he left playin' in the yard."

"He almost got Scooter drowned today."

Israel nodded and propped his elbow on the window frame. "And he's punishin' himself mighty bad about that, Bubba. Said up to prison, he always worried bout you boys swimmin' round that hole. Said he was so turned about, all he could think was 'I killed my boy . . . I killed my boy' and wont no good for nothin'. That a helpless feeling, Bubba. I know how it is." Then he smiled, "But he said you moved quick as greased lightnin' to get that boy out, and he was that proud."

Some of Bubba's bitterness slid away. He must not have told Israel about me slapping his hands away, the boy thought.

They pulled up to a square frame house. The red geraniums in tin cans on either side of the front stoop glowed in the headlights. "You wait here. I'll get Lily," Israel said as he stepped down from the truck.

Lily came to the door as Israel walked up the path. She listened to him, then took off her apron, patted the braids around her head with the flat of her hands, and disappeared into the house. In a moment, she came out and Bubba was glad to see she was carrying her " 'mergency bag." Lily had healing hands, and she always kept that bag full of medicines and such, ready to go help whoever needed it. They just might need something out of it if that daddemmed old doctor didn't show up.

Bubba slid out of the cupped seat to the higher center. The leather was cool, except where it had split and the stuffing pooched out. Lily's eyebrows were tight with worry as she opened the door, but they smoothed out when she saw Bubba. She and Israel got in, sandwiching him between them. The feel of her slender body was a comfort. "Hey, Bubba," she said.

"Hey."

"Fine. You all right?"

"I reckon."

Her hair glistened in the dim light as she settled her bag on her lap. As the engine started, she looked back to the truck bed. "Miss Queen didn't come along for a joyride?"

"We snuck off," Israel said.

"Huh, surprise me. That dog this here boy's shadow." She nudged Bubba, laughing. "Maybe that's how come she so black."

Their familiar teasing made Bubba feel better, till Israel said, "Not so spry as she was. Reckon she gettin' old, like the rest of us."

"She ain't old, Israel," Bubba objected. "Queen jumped right in that water today and would've pulled Scooter out if I hadn't."

"Is that so?" Israel said.

Now that Scooter's name had been mentioned, they all fell silent. The closer they got to home, the more Bubba's stomach tightened up. Lily's hands gripped her bag, and Israel leaned forward as if urging the truck faster as it bounced and jarred down the road.

As they turned into the path, Israel broke the silence with a sharp "Huh!" The headlights picked up a branch of the tree and the old tire swing, then landed full on the doctor's car, its chrome flashing needles of light back at them.

4

They found Jed waiting in the overstuffed chair by the lamp, his hands clasped tightly between his knees.

"The doctor had anything to say?" Israel asked.

Jed shook his head, "No word yet." A floorboard creaked as Lily shifted her weight. "Have a seat, Lily," he said. "You, too, Israel. Ain't no point in standin'."

Lily put down her bag and sat in the rocker on the

other side of the room, but Israel didn't move. Jed looked at him. "Sit down, Israel."

"I'm jes' fine, Mist Jed."

"No, you ain't." When Israel looked down at the floor, Jed said, "Don't you reckon we're past the point where you need to stand in my presence? Israel, you're my friend. This is my home. Sit."

The cane-bottomed chair protested as Israel lowered his bulk onto it. He perched on the edge, elbows on his knees, hands gripping his hat. Bubba, his legs suddenly weak, stepped back to sit on the padded stool behind him. Jed went back to studying the linoleum.

In the heavy silence, Bubba could tell Israel felt uncomfortable — almost like he wasn't putting his full weight on that seat. He'd sat in their kitchen a many a time, at ease with a cup of coffee, listening to the banter between Lily and Bubba's mama, but even Bubba knew coloreds weren't invited to sit in the house. He thought that was silly, and was glad that Jed had said what he did about him and Israel bein' friends. Why, if it hadn't been for Israel and Lily, he didn't know what they would've done. The Wades had been their mainstay while his daddy was gone. He wished Lily was in there now with Scoot instead of ole Doc Swinson. He wished for the sound of Scooter's jabber. He'd never tell him to hush again.

Suddenly Jed stood up. The bedroom door had

opened. As Israel and Lily got to their feet, a sudden sharp dread for Scooter made Bubba feel heavy all over, but he made himself stand.

Doctor Swinson came out, wiping his long-fingered hands on his handkerchief. Bubba wondered if the rust-colored stains on it were old blood or new. A mild surprise showed on the doctor's face at seeing Israel and Lily there in the sitting room, but he nodded to them. His eyes flicked past Jed to Ruby following him. "Just like I said, kids are hard to kill, Ruby. You just keep an eye on him tonight, make sure he hasn't passed out again." He looked at Bubba and answered the question in his eyes. "Your brother's gone be all right, boy. He just knocked the tar out of himself." Bubba nodded, his relief so great he couldn't speak. The doctor turned back to Ruby. "Let me know if anything changes. Otherwise, let him sleep. That's the Lord's way of healing."

"Thank you, Doctor," Ruby said.

"Glad it wasn't anything more serious. Children can scare the life out of you, I know, but they're tough. Like this one here," he gestured toward Bubba, "tough as they come. Ain't that so, Bubba?" The boy looked at the floor, his face reddening at the unexpected compliment. The doctor put an oversized hand under his chin, "But don't you let your brother swim round that deep hole anymore. You're older — you're supposed to know better." He said it to Bubba, but his eyes slid away toward Jed.

Ruby was watching Jed, too, holding her hands clasped together tightly, the palms rubbing against each other, the way she did when she was upset. Bubba suddenly realized the doctor had never spoken to Jed, and there were some grown-up things going on that he didn't understand. Doc Swinson was acting friendlier than usual, but all the time acting like Jed wasn't even there. In the silence, Bubba saw a slow red flush come up his father's neck, and for a moment he felt bad for him. But then he thought, If it hadn't been for him, Scooter wouldn't be in there so sick right now, and Doc Swinson wouldn't have to be here at all.

The doctor cleared his throat and said, "Well, I better be getting on. More sick folks around than you can shake a stick at. Summer doldrums, mostly. Fall weather'll perk 'em up — or maybe a good dose of your tonic is what they need, Lily."

Lily nodded in response, her eyes still on her hands clasped loosely in her lap. "Yes sir."

He patted Ruby on the shoulder. "Don't be worrying yourself now — Scoot's going to be fine. And you all can just pay me when you can." He glanced at Bubba. "I know you're good for it."

"That won't be necessary, Doctor." Jed bit off the words. "What's the charge?"

For the first time, Swinson looked right at him. "Five dollars. But I understand how it is with your family, Harkins. We've worked these things out before."

"Well, I'm home now, and there ain't no more need." Jed went to the bedroom and came back with the shiny gray jacket. He pulled out a crumpled ten-dollar bill.

Swinson's eyebrows went up. "Where'd you get this?"

"Never you mind. It's honest money."

Bubba gaped, and Ruby's expression was almost as shocked as the doctor's. Swinson fingered the bill.

"I'd appreciate the change, if you don't mind."

"Certainly, certainly." The doctor pulled a bill from his money clip. "Glad you intend to pull your own weight. You've got a fine wife and children here, and they had a mighty hard time with you away. For their sakes, I hope you can keep yourself straightened out."

Bubba thought the vein in his father's head was gone bust for sure. The two men glared at each other. Ruby stepped in, her voice soft but firm. "Doctor, we sure do 'preciate you comin'."

Swinson gave Jed a final scowl. "Glad to, Ruby. It's always a pleasure to deal with *you*." He left, and his car engine growled to life. The sound faded away.

Bubba watched his mama's puzzled eyes as she looked at Jed. He returned the look, unrepentant, and her gaze fell. She wiped her hands down her dress. "Well, thank the Lord that's over with," she said. "I don't know what got into that man. He's got no call to act that way. He knows full well Jed wouldn't build no still."

Israel glanced away as Lily tried to reassure her, "He didn't mean nothin'. That's just his way."

"Well, his way don't suit me one bit."

Bubba didn't see his mama's temper fly often, but she had her dander up now. Israel was turning his hat in his hands again like he was apt to wear it out. "Now Miss Ruby, don't you get yourself all riled up," he said. "Main thing is, Scooter's gone be just fine."

Jed put his arm around her. "It's all right, Ruby," he said, grinning. "I tell you, I would have given a hundred dollars to see the expression on that old rooster's face when I handed him that money."

"Look like his tail feathers got singed," said Lily.

"More like he'd had a dose of your tonic."

She slapped at the air. "What you say, Mist Jed? My tonic ain't that bad."

Bubba laughed with them but wasn't really sure why. Five dollars was a lot of money, and they had a passel of things they needed more. Doc Swinson would have waited. Where'd that money come from?

The laughter stopped short. "What did you say, boy?" Jed said.

He realized he'd said it out loud and swallowed. "I said, where'd you get all that money?"

Jed's words came out like ice cracking. "I earned that money fair and square. That's what you get for working your butt off for six years, making guano bags

33

and mattresses, that and that 'hope-it-don't-rain' suit, and a bus ticket home."

Nobody spoke, then Israel said, turning his hat again, " 'Spect that jute's mighty hard to work on."

"Like to tore my hands up. Never been so relieved in all my life when they transferred me to Virginia. At least there I got to get outside some."

The hat stopped. "Farm work?"

"Some. Mostly engine work — they found out I was good with machines."

Glad the attention was off him, Bubba caught his mama's eye. He tilted his head at the bedroom door. She nodded with a finger to her lips to be quiet, and he slipped inside.

She had turned the oil lamp beside the bed down to a tiny flickering flame, and the rest of the room was a circle of moving shadows. Scooter looked more natural now — arms and legs flung out across the bed, the covers twisted around his feet where he'd tried to kick them off. Relieved, Bubba moved closer. The bruise egg stood out blue on the boy's pale skin. That ole doctor hadn't even put a bandage on it.

Scooter's head moved on the pillow, and his lashes fluttered. Uh oh, Bubba thought, and held himself still. But Scoot's eyes opened and looked sleepily right at him. His lips moved. "Bubba?"

He bent close to hear. "Yeah?"

Scooter sighed. His eyelids drooped again, and the

whisper came even softer. "Me and Daddy had fun. You should have gone."

Bubba pulled back, blinking. Huh. Some fun. "Okay, Scooter, I'll go with you next time," he said softly, a promise to himself. Scooter snuggled back down and fell asleep again. Bubba's eyes suddenly stung. Thank the Lord he was gone be all right.

He left the door ajar for air and heard voices murmuring from outside, Israel's low bass and then Lily's soft drawl. He was glad they hadn't gone.

They were on the porch, enjoying the cool of the evening. His mama and Jed sat on the edge, Jed leaning against a post with Ruby sheltering in his arm. Seeing his mama sit with somebody like that took Bubba aback. "He doing all right, Bubba?" she asked. He nodded.

Israel pulled himself up with a grunt and slapped his hat on his head. "Well, it been some day. You all must be tired out. I know this body ready for rest, and I'm takin' it home."

Jed stood, too. "Ruby told me all the help you been. Want you to know I 'preciate it."

"Main help she had is standin' there beside you. Shoulda seen this boy take aholt. Done you proud."

Bubba felt his face redden, but Jed only nodded and held Israel with a steady look. "They couldn't have done it without you." He grasped Israel's shoulder and extended his other hand. "My thanks." For an instant, Israel seemed to hesitate, but then he shook it. Before Bubba knew it, the two men were in a bear hug, slapping each other on the back. When they moved apart, Israel's eyes glinted. "Good to have you back."

"Good to be back." Jed's voice was tight.

They headed for the truck, still talking softly. The warmth between them radiated out to the cool where Bubba was. Israel hadn't even said good night.

That night he couldn't sleep. The heat in the upstairs bedroom pressed down, and he tossed on the straw mattress, seeking a cool spot. Finally he crouched down by the window to catch some air. Downstairs, the clock chimed. He shifted as his knees started to hurt from the wood floor. The moon rode high, and the far cry of a whippoorwill broke the stillness of the whitened night as a breeze gentled his face. He rested his arm on the windowsill and stared at the black frame of trees until the moonlit field seemed to jump against it like a quivering silver band. He blinked, then blinked again. He nuzzled down and slept.

His eyelids flickered over dreams of sunlight shimmering on a road that turned to water, then moonlight lying across his bed, and his daddy sitting there like he had the night before he went away. His lips were moving, but Bubba couldn't hear, and Jed's eyes took on an indigo hue in their urgency to reach him.

Then the blue became Lily's dress, and she was

shucking corn in her kitchen with its row of herbs in snuff cans on the windowsill. "That thing just eatin' up this good corn!" she fussed at a worm, and Benjamin was holding his sides, laughing, as she threw it in the shucks to twist and curl in upon itself.

And it turned into Scooter curled up asleep, and a shadow came over him, like a gigantic foot about to stomp, and he screamed, and his daddy's voice shouted, "I told you to take care of your mama and the baby, boy. Now see what you done!" and then Bubba cried out.

5

Scooter was up and running before the knot on his head had gone down. As the weeks passed, most times Bubba looked, the boy was tagging after Jed. That man had come right in and taken over, and treated Bubba like he didn't know nothin'. Seemed like nothing he did pleased his father, and not much Jed did pleased Bubba. What with Ruby pushing Jed at him and Scoot yapping Daddy did this and Daddy did that, Bubba felt beset on all sides, so he spent what free time he had at Israel's. Home was a stranger's house now, and the unchanged routines at the Wades' had been a relief. But here was Lily saying he should quit worrying and enjoy being a kid again like Scooter. "Huh. Reckon I don't want to act like I got no more sense than that," Bubba snorted, "closer'n a sticktight to Daddy all the time."

She was taking advantage of the cooler day to iron. As he sat at the kitchen table with a tall glass of iced tea, a soft breeze rustled in the honeysuckle bush outside the window, and he fancied he could feel a touch of crisp autumn air in the sweet fragrance.

Lily gripped the humped-over handle of the flatiron with a folded cloth as she lifted it from the stove. She held it close to her cheek to test for heat, then looked at him with a questioning eyebrow raised. "What you mean?"

"Ought to remember who it was almost killed him."

"Huh!" she hurled a quick spit at the iron plate. The drops bubbled and danced, but she double-checked by spitting again on her fingers and touching the iron with a dancing pat of her own. "You still blamin' your daddy for that? Everybody entitled to one mistake, Bubba." Her iron twisted and turned across a dampened shirt, leaving a smooth track behind. For a moment, she was almost hidden in the cloud of steam that rose. A hot flour-starch smell filled the room. He traced a pattern on his sweating glass. "Tell the truth now," she went on. "Reckon you just a mite jealous Scooter took to him so fast?" He didn't answer. "You miss him, don't you?"

"That little worrywart?" Bubba snorted. "I just don't want him to get hisself killed is all."

Her hand fell on his shoulder. "Bubba, look at me." He looked straight into her brown eyes with their tiny red veins tracing the yellowish whites, seeing only the warm understanding there. He swallowed. Maybe he shouldn't have come today. She knew him too well. "Son, your daddy love that boy. He gone look after him and your mama, and you, too, if'n you let him." She went back and resumed ironing. "You is out of prison, just as sure as your daddy is. His the responsibility now." She looked at him sideways, "You 'spect that chaineyball tree still hold you?"

He ducked his head at her good-natured teasing. When he was little, that tree had been his favorite place. The branches twined to make a natural seat up high, hidden by the canopy of leaves — he'd thought.

"You think you hidin' so good, but your mama and daddy knew to listen more than look. I remember clear as day," she chuckled, "you asittin' up in that tree, swingin' your legs and whistlin' up a storm."

"I don't even know if I can still whistle."

"Then high time you findin' out."

"Lily, I ain't got time . . ."

She whirled around. "Ain't you heard a thing I said?" She put her hand on her hip. "What you 'spect gone happen to you, you don't give yourself room to grow and learn? You passed your grade last year by the skin of your teeth. Now you can put your mind to learnin', and that there learnin' will set you free. Else you gone end up just where you at now — day in, day out, chores, chores, chores. They's more to life than that." She waved toward the window. "Look around you for onct. The good Lord made a beautiful world, but I bet you ain't looked at it good in I don't know how long."

"But Lily . . ."

She held up her hand and went on, "I know you ain't had much choice up to now, for folks is got to eat and make do. But now things is different. Doggone it, Bubba, you got worry lines, and you only twelve! Leave go!" She picked up the other iron that had been heating, muttering, "Tears me and Israel up to see you turnin' into an old man 'fore your time." Her iron thumped against the table.

Lord, wouldn't he like to have it off him? But he couldn't just push his family off onto somethin' he didn't know could hold them up. She just didn't understand. He got up and put his glass on the sink. "Well, I best get on home. Thanks for the tea."

"Anytime." She kept ironing.

He waited a minute, but she didn't look up. "Well, bye." He was almost out the door when he heard:

"Don't I get my hug?"

He looked back. Lily's feelings were right in her eyes, like she was sorry. Lordamercy, he hadn't hugged her goodbye since he was a little thing. He put his arm around her waist awkwardly.

"There now," she laughed, hugging him back. "First lesson in being a boy again. Feels right good, don't it?" His throat was so tight he could only nod.

In the woods, sunlight flowed like honey down through the bright orange sassafras leaves. A cardinal landed almost in front of his nose, its leathery claws gripping the low branch. He saw the silky red feathers in its crown, even the black rim around its eye. He watched until it fluttered away. Suddenly Bubba realized the woods were full of birds, flitting from branch to branch, chirping and chattering at each other. Wonder why I always thought the woods was so quiet? he thought. Maybe Lily was right.

As he broke from the trees, the sun slanted across the field, the pines casting shadows on the goldenrod swaying in the cooling air where corn should have been. He looked up at an eagle cruising the sky, swooping in great circles on the wind. Wonder what it'd be like to be so free and able to fly way up like that, just lookin' out for your own self? he thought. Taking a deep breath, he spread his arms full length, let out a shout and ran. Dipping and swaying, he cut a path through the weeds, the yellow blooms snapping back, exploding pollen into the air. A golden haze marked his trail as he stopped abruptly, feeling foolish. He brushed his clothes and sighed. Lily means well, but she's wrong. Too late to be a care-for-nothin' now.

He was no sooner home than Scooter came careening around the house. "Bubba! Come on, we got to get cleaned up. We're goin' to town."

"What you mean? This ain't Saturday."

"It don't matter. Daddy said Israel's got to see bout fixing a wheel, so we're all gone go. And he done give us money to get haircuts for school!" He held out his hand. "See? He said for you to hold it."

Fifty cents? Didn't that ole man know they needed to save every bit with Scooter and him both needin' shoes? But he put the warm coins in his bib pocket.

Bubba leaned against the cool metal side of the truck bed. Through the dust tail rising behind them, the sumac leaves along the road glowed red even through their gray coating. He stretched and moved the sharp points of his mama's scissors in his pocket away from his skin. The women were crowded in front with Israel, but Jed and Scooter sat train-fashion across from Bubba, the boy holding between his legs the basket of eggs Ruby planned to trade. Against the broken wheel, two chickens lay, legs trussed and a burlap sack over their heads, quiet as if they were already dead.

The truck lurched to a stop in front of the general store. On either side, the sidewalks stretched all but deserted in the sun, with only a few cars angled in to the curb. A colored lady walked down the street, umbrella held high to shade her from the hot sun. Under the willow tree, a dog followed its tail and lay down.

A square-built man dressed in a three-piece suit and a collar high enough to look like it would choke came out of the store and saw them. "Well, I'll be blessed if it ain't Miss Ruby! What you in town for today?" he said. Bubba wrinkled his nose. Ole Preacher Satterthwaite was always blessin' and praisin'. He never could say "Hi do" like regular folks.

Ruby smiled, but before she could answer, Jed stood up in the back of the truck with the trussed chickens. The preacher's eyes flared wide, then he turned his back and walked stiff-legged away. Jed stood there, a chicken in each hand and his jaw slack.

"Wont that the preacher?" Scooter asked.

"Was it now? I didn't see nobody," Jed answered, his smile rigid. He handed the birds to Bubba and went back to unloading the truck. The hurt on his mama's face made Bubba look away. He hadn't expected the preacher to act so, even if he was a real strong temperance man.

Charles Proctor appeared behind the flyspecked screen door. "Now Israel, you know you need to pull that truck of yours around the back to do your tradin'."

Israel pulled off his hat. "Yessuh, Mist Charles, but this here ain't my stuff. It belong to Miss Ruby."

Charles stepped out, the screen squealing. He was dry and spare, the bones in his arms sharp angles under his white freckled skin. "Well, hey there, Ruby. Didn't see you at first. And you brung your boys, too. Need school clothes, I 'spect, less'n they gone wear knee pants." He laughed at his own wit. The boys exchanged a disgusted look: Grownups. Abruptly, the storekeeper got quiet as Jed came around the truck to join them. The giggles of some children playing at the side of the store caught Charles's notice, and he snapped, "You jigaboos get away from here!" They scattered, and finally he said, "Hey, Jed. I see you're back."

"I'm back. How you do, Charles?"

"Fine, fine." The storekeeper ran his fingers through his few strands of sandy hair. Bubba heard a rustling noise. Several men were standing inside the store doorway, and ole Tom Sly had his nose pressed up against the window, peering out between the Tuberose Snuff posters. Bubba looked away, his ears hot.

Turning back to Ruby, Charles said, "Got some apples, I see. Fine eatin'. And you brung eggs, too. Good, good. Townfolks can't seem to get enough of them good country eggs." Bubba had never heard the man jabber so. His back tickled like all them eyes were boring into it, but he knew they were staring at his father, not him.

"You reckon we can do some business, Charles?"

Charles jumped at Jed's voice. Like a snake had

44

spoke, Bubba thought. He watched his father uneasily. He better be careful, he's walking a line. The storekeeper was used to dealing with his mama and could even refuse to do business with Jed. And all them men standin' there watching, and not one coming out to say a word of welcome home. Just watching. Now his daddy was back, Bubba had hoped they would forgive and forget. But that wont to be — not with the preacher and Doc Swinson and maybe even Mr. Charles turning their backs. Nobody wanted to cross them men.

But Charles said, "Reckon we can, long as you're as honest in your dealin's as your wife here."

Jed's lips narrowed. Scooter jumped out of the truck and pulled on Bubba's arm. "Can we go now?"

Ruby seemed glad enough to break the tension. "You two hurry. No dawdlin', now."

Scooter was gone before she finished, running toward the storefront where a red-and-white barber pole spun lazily. His prideful streak coming out, Bubba nodded to the storekeeper and then to the men in the doorway. They nodded back, still silent. Now he really felt their eyes on him, and he made it a point to walk straight and not go running off like some little kid.

His brother was almost to the barbershop. "Hey, Scoot, wait."

"Hurry up, Bubba. I ain't never had a real haircut in a barbershop before."

Bubba hated to disappoint him, but it was shoes or a

45

store-bought haircut, and shoes were more important. He fingered the scissors in his pocket.

They ambled back down the street, Bubba deliberately loitering. He didn't think he'd done too bad a job on Scooter's hair, but he didn't like the way the boy grinned when he looked at him. A car nosing in to park looked like it was going to run them over until the curb stopped it with a jerk. They jumped back. "Darned ole fool," Bubba muttered.

"Derned ole fool," echoed Scooter.

"What's that, boys?"

Bubba turned. He hadn't seen Ole Raggey get out with the doctor. Scooter's mouth fell open as he looked up at the man in the neatly pressed suit. "We didn't say nothin'," Bubba mumbled, uncomfortable under the stern eye. From his crewcut hair down to his spit-shined shoes, Oscar Raggenbotham still had the bearing of the military man he'd been twenty years before. Everybody at school dreaded having him for a teacher. Bubba would have him again this year.

"How you boys doin' today?" Doc Swinson said.

They nodded, then Bubba saw Ole Raggey looking at him hard. He swallowed. "Just fine, sir."

"That head doing all right?" Swinson rubbed at Scooter's hair, and the boy ducked away. Chuckling, he said to Raggenbotham, "Harkins's other boy. Scooter will be in first grade this year."

Raggenbotham's lips slid back. "How nice. I shall

look forward to seeing this young man." In an undertone he added, "Nothing like his father, I hope?"

The doctor brushed the question away. "No, no. *Both* these are fine boys. Take after their mama." Looking closer at Bubba, he pulled out his glasses. His eyebrows went up. "What have you boys been up to?"

"Got a haircut for school," Bubba said.

"Do tell," Doc grinned. "Guess if you got money enough for haircuts, it won't be long before you can pay me that fifty cents you're still owing."

Bubba looked the doctor in the eye, but as he did, it seemed the two quarters in his bib pocket burned. They did owe it. With a sigh, he pulled out the coins. "Reckon I better go on and pay you now."

"Well, isn't that fine?" Swinson beamed. "That settles us up all fair and square."

Bubba felt like kicking the office door as it closed behind the two men.

"That man gone be my teacher?" Scooter asked.

"Naw. Mr. Raggenbotham teaches the big boys."

"He looks mean."

"He's just a teacher." But Ole Raggey was mighty strict and wouldn't hesitate to whip somebody did he think they needed it. The kids hated him. And from what he'd heard at the store, grownups didn't hold him in high regard neither. He'd heard Mr. Charles say Raggey ought not talk so poormouth, what with him buying up all that land when folks had to sell or be

47

sold up for taxes. And Henry Howell had leaned back in his chair, saying, "Yeah, Oscar Raggenbotham might as well run for sheriff, he at the sales so much," and Mr. Charles went "Huh," and all the men had laughed. Then Tom Sly had said, "He can buy up all creation if he wants to, but him and his like best stay out of *this* county."

His mama was waiting on the bench outside the store, her worn leather pocketbook clutched to her chest. She was watching a butterfly flit over a stand of purple mistflowers. Oh, she was somewhat pretty with her yellow hair, was his mama. Especially when she sat still like that, her mind off somewhere and her green eyes glowing. Then she spotted him, "Landamercy, Bubba. Is that the best that barber can do? You look a sight!"

Jed came down the street. Puzzled, he looked at Scooter squatting in the dirt as he watched the butterfly. "Thought you boys were gone get a haircut."

Scooter looked up. "Our hair's been cut, Daddy."

"For sure ain't no barber done that."

The boy grinned. "Bubba cut it."

"That was a dern fool thing to do. Didn't I give you boys fifty cents so you could get your hair cut decent for school? You savin' it for candy, that's too bad." He put his hand out to Bubba. "Fork it over."

"He can't give it back. It's gone," Scooter said.

"Money don't just get gone," Jed snapped. "It's spent or it's saved or it's lost. You tellin' me you lost it?

Don't you know how hard money is to come by? I'da thought better of you, Bubba."

Bubba's head came up, his lips tight. For sure he knew how hard money was to come by — none better.

Ruby stepped in. "Now both of you calm down just a minute, and let's see can we get to the bottom of this."

"I'll get to the bottom of it, Ruby. This here boy ain't got too big for me to whip."

White-faced, Scooter glared up at his father. "You ain't gone whip Bubba. He ain't done nothin' bad. He had to pay somebody."

Jed looked down at him. "Explain yourself."

Scooter took a deep breath. "Ole Doc Swinson bout runned over us with a mean man named Mr. Raggybottom and I thought he was gone be my teacher, but he ain't, and Doc started talkin' bout fifty cents we owed, and Bubba had to pay him off." He stuck his chin out. "And I didn't want no barber cuttin' my hair all off anyways."

"Watch who you sassin', boy."

Ruby put her hand on Jed's arm. "Is this true, Bubba?" she asked in a quiet voice. He nodded. "When we owe the doctor any money from?"

He glanced away. "From when you were so sick last winter. I'd bout paid him off but for that fifty cents."

"I guess we ain't got nothin' to say then, Jed. The boy was only doin' what I taught him to do. First what's owin' gets paid, then everything else after."

"Doggone it, Ruby. Them haircuts was somethin' I wanted to do for my boys." He looked at Scooter. "You say somethin' bout Raggenbotham being your teacher?"

"No sir," Scooter shook his head hard. "Mr. Raggy-bottom gone be Bubba's teacher."

"His name is Raggenbotham, son, and be sure you got it right. He don't like to be miscalled." He looked at Ruby. "I hoped he'd be long gone by now." She shook her head, her lips tight.

Then she said, "I'll see what I can do with those haircuts when we get home. We'd best get our shoppin' done 'fore Israel and Lily get back."

"You and the boys go on in." Jed sat on the bench. "I'll wait out here so's I can see Israel when he gets ready to put that wheel back in the truck."

"You don't want to come in?"

He avoided her look. "Best not. He'll need help."

"What you think best," she nodded, and went up the steps into the store, Scooter right behind her. Jed stretched out his long legs. Bubba didn't like to leave his father there, and he didn't like it that Jed wouldn't go in. Wouldn't no bunch of cold-faced men be able to stop his real daddy from going into no store.

He shrugged his shoulders and went on inside.

6

Scooter's birthday finally came, although he'd fussed for days that he thought it never would. The boy's excitement was infectious, and now as Bubba ducked his head under the pump to rinse off for supper, he smiled, remembering how Scoot had gone full speed all day in a rush to get his chores done, even gathering the eggs without complaining, something he hated, for he was always slipping on the chicken droppings. Bubba grabbed the flour-sack towel off the nail and scrubbed dry, then looked in the cracked, stained mirror to finger-comb his hair. He paused to rub Queen's silken ears, admiring the long shadows across the dirt-packed yard. The chinaberry tree fanned out, hiding mysteries in its canopy, and he felt a sudden yearning to climb into its branches. He remembered how it was, the cool whispering leaves, the hard chaineyball pods forming, bitter to the taste, and sometimes a bird's nest to be kept for treasure.

He picked up the brown paper package on the shelf. He sure had wanted to get Scoot some shoes for his birthday, but he hadn't raised enough money yet, so he'd just have to make do with the homemade ball and the penny candy. Pretty sorry pickin's for a boy turning six, Bubba thought. He wished he had something special to give. His hand stilled on Queen's head. He knew what he'd do. As quick as the thought came, he hurried across the porch back into the house.

By the time he came into the kitchen, the rest of them were already at the table. "Bout time you got here, boy," Jed said. "Your mama works hard to put us a good meal on the table. Least you can do is be here on time and not let it get cold."

Bubba slid onto the bench next to his brother, his mouth watering at the good smell of squirrel stew. As they held hands to say the blessing, he felt the pulse in Jed's firm dry hand, and Scooter's lay in his relaxed and loose, like a small animal's.

After they'd finished eating, Scooter couldn't wait to get at his presents. He opened Bubba's first. The twine ball rolled out onto the table, and the boy cradled it in his hands, his eyes shining. "Will you teach me to play ball like the big boys do?" Bubba nodded. Then Scoot opened the candy, and finally the hardest of all to give, the knife his daddy had given Bubba before he went away. It was a good one, with a fine bone handle, and he'd always felt proud when the other boys at school looked at his knife with wanting eyes. As Scooter pulled it out, his face went still. Bubba waited for him to say something. Maybe he didn't like it, and he had given it for nothing.

Scooter rubbed his fingers across the design on the

handle in his hand. Then he looked up. "For me?" Bubba nodded. "But it's your special knife."

"Well, now it's your special knife. And mind you take good care of it."

Jed looked at him across the table. "That the knife I gave you?" he asked quietly.

Bubba nodded. "Figured a boy reachin' six was big enough to have a knife of his own. Boy needs a knife," he added, defensively.

Jed didn't speak, but his mama's hand touched his shoulder. "Mighty fine thing for you to do, Bubba." He looked down at his hands, missing the knife already.

From then on, it seemed like nothing went right. Bubba's special presents were forgotten when Scooter opened his daddy's gift — a wooden set of cowboys and Indians Jed had carved for him while away, every feature sharp, each feather clearly etched, the wrinkles in the clothes a thin groove. Scooter hugged his daddy. "This is the best birfday I ever had! I got me a knife and a ball and a special bunch of cowboys and Injuns that my daddy made all by himself," he hugged him even tighter, "and I got me my daddy, and I'm *six!*"

Bubba stared at the backs of the toy figures, the man and boy beyond, and at his knife lying forgotten on the table, and his heart felt like a weight, in spite of the fake smile he kept on his face.

Bubba was glad to see Israel's truck pull up under the tree. He'd been up there ever since supper, brooding while he watched the dusk settle over the land. The call of the whippoorwill had only made his loneliness worse. As Israel and Lily got out of the truck, Jed came to the door. "Hey there," he said.

"Hear tell there's a birthday boy round here. Wonder who it can be?" Israel said.

"It's me, it's me," Scooter yelled as he barreled off the porch into Israel's arms.

"Mmph," Israel grunted. "Seems to me you got heavier than you was yesterday. Reckon you growin' up."

Scooter squirmed down and ran over to Lily. She gave him a swirl-around right underneath the tree. They were both laughing, Scooter with his head flung back, and Bubba had to grin at the boy's expression when he looked up and saw him. "Hey, Bubba, what you doin' up there? Israel and Lily's here."

Bubba swung down. He was tired of feeling shut out anyway. Now maybe Scooter wouldn't be so wrapped up in his daddy and those cowboys and Indians.

"First time I seen you in that tree in many a day," Lily said.

"Found out I could still get up there." They shared a secret smile.

Israel pulled a long, odd-shaped package from the truck. Bubba knew it was a bat he'd made from ash wood.

"You all come on in," Ruby said, slapping her arm.

"I swan, I don't think these skeeters are ever goin' to get gone. We'll get eat up we stay out here talkin'."

"I got some chores to finish up first," Jed said. "Won't take but a minute."

"I'll go with you," Israel said, following him.

Scooter looked at his mama. "Does that mean I have to wait to open my present?"

She nodded. "Your daddy won't be long."

In the kitchen, Scooter dumped the present on the table and stared at it, his face in his hands. Lily teased. "You gone stare a hole in that paper, boy?"

"What'd Israel have to go with Daddy for?"

"Chile, you gone learn. Where your daddy goes, Israel gone be there, too, or at least close by. When them boys was growin' up, they was thick as thieves."

"You mean when they was bout big as me?"

Lily nodded. "Since just about your size. Where you see one, you see the other." She laughed, " 'Cept the time your daddy landed in that hole."

Scooter's eyes widened. "What hole?" he asked.

She clucked her tongue. "Well, you quit bein' a squirmtail and come over here, I might just tell you."

The boy climbed in her lap, and Bubba smiled. Scoot had walked right into another one of her stories, just like she'd meant him to. He settled down to listen.

Lily put her arm around Scooter. "Well, it was a long time ago. Your daddy just about your age, Bubba.

He still just a little scrawny thing, but Israel, he'd bout come to his full size, and they was a sight, I tell you, that big colored boy and that little ole white one. But they like brothers." Her eyes took on a faraway look as she remembered. "This here day, they gone huntin' to Mist Farley's place. He'd told them to stay out, but they didn't listen. The dogs was abarkin', runnin' this away and that, and your daddy was leadin', with Israel right behind, when all of a sudden your daddy weren't there no more. Israel said he let out a yelp like them dogs, and then he was gone slam out of sight."

"What'd Israel do?" Bubba asked.

"Oh, you know Israel — he a cautious man. He ease up that path, and sure enough, that ground went down. He was right on the edge of a deep hole, and your daddy was down at the bottom, with his leg broke and no way out. Israel said he down so far, he couldn't see but the top of his yaller hair. Said good thing he wont colored, or nobody woulda ever found him!" she chuckled.

"Must have been mighty deep," Bubba said.

She nodded. "Old well. You see, Mist Farley knew that old cover had rotted out. That's why he told them boys to stay out of his woods."

Scooter couldn't wait. "What happened then?"

"Well, Israel told your daddy he be right back, and he lit out runnin' to our house." She smiled, remembering, "Israel didn't even know I was alive then, but I knew he was. A fine-lookin' boy, yessir."

"And then?" Bubba urged her back to the story.

"Well, he come runnin' into our yard and ast my daddy for some rope, said his friend fell down a hole and he had to get him up. Well, Daddy got the rope and a lantern — it was gettin' dark about then — and off they went. And I wont far behind. My mama woulda tore my hide up did she know, but where Israel gone be, there I gone be, too."

"I can believe that," Ruby said, smiling.

"And then what?" Scooter said.

"Well, we got down into them woods, and it gettin' black as pitch, and I sure was glad my daddy brought that lantern. I stuck close as a burr, and he didn't say a thing." She widened her eyes as she shook her head. "Ooooeee, it got darker and darker, and I thought for sure we was all gone get eat up by snakes or bears or what all. Israel was goin' ahead like he could see in the dark, callin' 'Jed? . . . Jed . . . ?' and now and then whistlin', till finally we could hear a tiny whistle, like from far off. Now we close on him, so Israel, he drop to his knees and inch his way up, and Daddy tryin' to lean over to swing that lantern in front of him so's he could see. Then that whistle come again, closer, but real thin-like. Israel stretch out flat on his belly, feelin' his way."

Bubba glanced at Scooter. He was listening with his mouth half-open, hanging on her every word.

"He reached that hole, and them leaves were just aslidin' down in that lantern light. Then Israel jump up so fast like to scared me to death, and he grabbed that rope outten my daddy's hands. Quick as a wink, he had one end tied round his foot and the other round an old stump. My daddy holt on, too, and Israel went headfirst down in that pit. I thought sureforeGod he gone fall in, and me just holdin' my breath . . ." Bubba realized he'd been holding his, too.

"Then I sees him start to wiggle his way back. His muscles bulged up so bad strainin', his shirt ripped right open. Here he come, still workin' his way back, gruntin', and my daddy goin' 'Easy, easy.' First thing I knows, here comes his arms up, and Mist Jed's hands holdin' on for dear life, awrapped around Israel's elbows, and them arms twined together, brown and white . . ." She closed her eyes, shaking her head. "I can still see it to this day."

Taking a deep breath, she went on. "And then there's Mist Jed's head and shoulders, and my daddy reachin' over and grabbin' him under his armpit. Between the two of them, they got Mist Jed out and lay him down. Israel, he was breathin' so hard I thought his lungs gone bust, and Mist Jed was white white — whiter'n I ever seen him before, and his leg twisted right crook-sided. I could tell he was hurtin' somewhat bad. I didn't know then what I knows now, so I couldn't do a thing, and it hurt my heart, I can tell you, just to stand there and watch him suffer so." She looked at Ruby. "Reckon that's why I learned the healin' arts. Knew right then I couldn't stand by, had

58

to be doin' somethin' to help." Ruby nodded her understanding.

"Go on," Scooter insisted.

"Well, you know yourself, Israel ain't no man to let grass grow under his feet. He untied hisself — that rope right bloody where it chafed him — and picked up your daddy gentle as you please and carried him out of them woods to where he could get some help."

Bubba could see it all — the dark woods, the old well, the leaves sliding in, and the brown hands and the white ones hooked up together.

"Them two been bound up together ever since," Lily said softly. "They closer than blood kin. Ain't nothin' one wouldn't do for the other, and that's a fact. They grown-up, but they still the same as them two boys. They's a little older, but that make no difference. That love the same."

Just then the two men came in the door. Bubba, brought back to the present, looked up and knew one of the men wasn't the same.

7

The night before school started, Ruby and Jed told Scooter. When Bubba went up to bed, he had a feeling something was going on, for his mama stalled Scooter downstairs. He lay in the bed watching the flickering shadows and hearing his parents' murmuring voices from downstairs, and from time to time Scooter's high voice. Questions. That boy was always good for questions.

But Scoot was silent when he finally came up. As he slipped into bed, Bubba blew out the kerosene lamp and snuggled down. He didn't have to wait long.

"Bubba?"

"Yeah?"

"Daddy's been in jail."

"Yeah, I know."

There was a long silence. "Bubba, what's a still?"

"Somethin' they use to make corn likker like grown-ups drink to get drunk."

"You mean like Tom Sly?"

Bubba nodded in the dark. "Like Tom Sly."

"Daddy says he didn't build no still, so how come he had to go to jail?"

"Folks make mistakes, is all. Now go on to sleep. You got a big day tomorrow." Scooter sighed. Bubba waited until he heard the boy's regular breathing, then he too sighed, and let himself go to sleep.

The next day, the boys made their way along the road, their book bags each holding a new yellow pencil and an Indian Head writing tablet, and metal lunch pails swinging from their hands. Beside the ditches, spider-webs stretched across the bushes, cradling the early dew, and pink morning glories twined up the dried cornstalks. Seemed a shame to go back to school when it still felt like summer, Bubba thought. But the signs of fall were there: trees speckling with color, cornstalks waiting to be gathered for fodder, cool nights, and morning fog rising in wide bands from the fields.

Scooter clumped along beside him in Bubba's hand-me-down brogans, while he went barefoot, his feet already filmed with gray dust. He'd stalled his mama from buying him new shoes — just getting their new overalls and such had almost used up her garden money. He'd raise the money somehow. Maybe Israel would even lend him a trap. If he could get some furs to trade, then maybe Scoot and him both could have new shoes.

He dreaded what the day might bring. He could handle any teasin' for being the only one barefoot, but he just hoped to God they wouldn't give Scooter no mess about his daddy. He didn't think the boy could take the other kids shoutin' "Prison kid, prison kid," like he'd had to until he learned to give as well as get. Now his father was home, it might start all over again. Smart alecks like Grady Ferrell liked to pick on the new kids anyway.

His stomach knotted when he saw the schoolyard

ahead, then he realized Scooter was nowhere in sight. Ashamed of the relief he felt at the delay, he hurried back to look for him. Sure enough, there he was, hidden by the bend in the road, poking a stick in the ditch. Bubba hollered, "Scooter Harkins, get yourself up here!"

The boy threw the stick away and came at an awkward run, his book bag bouncing. "Bubba, there was the biggest butterfly you ever did see. All orange and black."

"Well, come on to school, and maybe you can learn all about them butterflies and bugs you like so good. Won't do to be late your first day."

When they came out into the sun, the other kids stopped their talking. Bubba felt the small hand tighten in his and gave it a reassuring squeeze. As they crossed the silent schoolyard, he ignored the rocks and cinders stabbing his feet. Scooter held on with an iron grip, his sweat slicking their hands.

"Ho, Bubba," a voice called from the far corner. It was Jimmy Leon Woodsley. Bubba waved back. The chattering began again, and as they went through the door, he could have sworn he heard someone saying something about shoes and laughing.

In the classroom, last year's smell of chalk dust and sour wool was gone. The air was crisp with polish and soap, but the names gouged in the desks were still there, permanently stained with dirt and oil from sweating hands, and so were the paper spitballs glued to the ceiling. The stove in the middle of the big room was shining, the blackboard washed, and the sting of fresh lye struck beyond his nose to kindle a reluctant excitement at school starting. Mr. Tetley was setting out books at a precise angle on each desk. Bubba was always surprised at how timid the teacher was outside the schoolroom, but he'd always liked him. He'd been a big help when his daddy had first gone away.

"Ah, Bubba, good to see you back," Tetley smiled. He glanced down at Bubba's feet, then discreetly looked away at Scooter. "And what have we here?"

"This here," Bubba started, but then corrected himself. "This is my brother Aubrey, Mr. Tetley, but we call him Scooter for short."

Tetley smiled at the boy. "Welcome to Little Branch School, Master Scooter Harkins. I hope you learn what you love here, and love what you learn."

Bubba grinned. Mr. Tetley said that to all the kids, and every one of them thought he was saying it just to them. He meant it, too. Bubba sure wished he still had Mr. Tetley for a teacher, instead of Ole Raggey.

"Yes sir," Scooter replied, sticking out his hand for all the world like a man grown.

Tetley held back a smile as he shook the boy's hand. "Well, Scooter, how would you like to help me ring the bell to get those vagrants into the classroom?"

As they went out, Scooter asked, "Mr. Tetley, what's

a vagrant?" and Bubba's smile widened. At last, somebody else could deal with Scooter's questions.

Yelling and laughing, the kids spilled out onto the yard at recess. Bubba took his time coming out.

"Hey boy, ain't you got no tow sacks you can put on them feet? I can smell 'em all the way over here." That was redheaded Grady Ferrell.

"Yeah, Bubba, why don't you go stick 'em in the water bucket and give us some relief?" Jarvis Badden always echoed Grady, but he was mean in his own right, with narrow eyes and a narrower nose.

"Thinks he's too good to talk, now his daddy's home."

"Huh, some daddy," Jarvis said.

Bubba stared at them. Jarvis's eyes dropped first.

"Whoo-ee, look at them mean eyes," Grady mocked. "Just a chip off the old block."

"Hush your mouth, Grady Ferrell." Thora, Grady's twin sister, stood there, her hands on her hips and her black-stockinged legs set firm. "If you ain't careful, Bubba's gone knock your block off. Maybe you forgot that whippin' he gave you coupla years back?"

"Aw, we was just kiddin' around," Grady said.

"I don't see anybody laughin'."

Scooter ran up. "Hey, Bubba, I think I'm gone like school. Did you hear me ring the bell?"

Bubba kept his eyes on Grady, mentally daring him to say anything about his daddy in front of Scooter. But

Grady looked away and Bubba breathed again. "That's fine, Scoot. I told you Mr. Tetley was real nice. Thora, this here's my little brother, Scooter."

"Hey, Scooter. Welcome to the chain gang." Bubba shot her a look and she colored up, her freckles almost lost in the flush. "I mean, glad to have you at school, that's all." She gave Grady a shove, pushing him and Jarvis across the yard. Bubba was glad to see them go.

"What'd she get red like that for, Bubba? She say somethin' wrong?"

"Naw, she just likes to talk tough. Most kids like school, but they like to put on they don't."

"That's crazy. School is fun. I'm gone see if Mr. Tetley will let me ring the bell again." Scooter dodged around a group of girls singing "Ring-Around-the-Rosie," and ran back inside.

Bubba didn't see Scooter again until lunchtime, and he was late getting out for that. Mr. Raggenbotham had kept him in about not wearing shoes, but he hadn't had much to say when Bubba told him he didn't have any. He'd fussed some about school rules, but there wont much he could do, less'n he wanted to buy some out of his own pocket. Huh, not likely, Bubba thought. Still, he didn't like to see him put out. Ole Raggey sure could get mean when people didn't do like he thought they should.

Leaning against the rough brick wall of the

schoolhouse, Bubba peeled the soft skin off his sweet potato. From the corner of his eye, he saw Grady talking to some of the smaller children. The kids scattered, giggling, and Grady's face got a look that Bubba knew from long past meant he was up to something. He took a bite of the potato, but it lost its taste when he heard voices chanting from the back of the schoolhouse. He scrambled up, knocking his lunch pail over into the dirt. He'd heard that chant before. Blindly, he tossed the potato away and cut across the yard. The voices got louder as he turned the corner:

> "Jailbird, jailbird,
> That's the warden's fav'rite word.
> One, two, three, four,
> Here he comes to shut the door."

Scooter was jumping rope, with a boy and a girl at each end of the line. A group of kids were chanting:

> "Clink, clank, golly gee,
> Now he's thrown away the key."

"Look at me, Bubba! Look at me!" Scooter called with a wide grin. But the chant continued relentlessly on, and Bubba was too late:

> "Five, six, seven, eight,
> Here's the guard to shut the gate!"

The rope pulled tight. Caught in midjump, Scooter fell into the gravel as the children squealed with laughter. He looked up at Bubba, tears welling, a raw scrape on his cheek. Bubba started forward, but he tripped and went down. He turned and saw Grady sniggering, Jarvis slapping him on the back.

"Hard to walk with no shoes, ain't it, Bubba?"

"Yeah, only no-counts go barefoot," Jarvis added.

His shin smarted. "You put those kids up to that!"

"Who, me?" Grady spread his arms wide. "It's just an old playground game. Whatsa matter, you got somethin' against jail . . ."

Bubba's fist stopped the word cold. When Grady tried to say something else, he hit him again. Scoot's standin' right there, Bubba thought. Determined to stop Grady's mouth, he got him down on the ground. Jarvis headed their way, fists balled.

Scooter shouted, "You leave my brother alone! Two 'gainst one ain't fair!" and knocked him behind the knees.

The kids took up another chant, "Fair fight! Fair fight!" But Jarvis only stumbled and came on, with Scooter still hanging on to his pants leg.

Then Grady had Bubba down, gouging, scratching, hitting. Bubba strained to grab hold of the boy's arms. He heard Jarvis yell, and then someone else landed on top of them. Thora was riding Grady's back, her red hair glowing from the sun behind, and a battle gleam lit her eyes. "Let him go, Grady, let him go!" she yelled, grabbing his hair and pulling his head back. It was the opening Bubba had been waiting for. He socked Grady so hard, pain shot up his arm. Grady screamed and rolled off, holding his bloody mouth. Bubba struggled to his feet. A hand reached out to steady him. "You all right?" Thora asked.

"Fine," he said. They exchanged smiles of victory. Suddenly shy, he looked away. " 'Preciate your help."

" 'Tweren't nothin'. He had it comin'," she said. She wasn't looking directly at him, either.

"We beat 'em, Bubba, you and me, we beat the tar outten 'em!" Scooter exulted, still standing guard over Jarvis, who held his hand against his bleeding leg.

"Mean little kid like to bit my leg off."

Thora tossed her head. "Oh, shut your whining, Jarvis. You boys ain't gone fight fair, you ought not 'spect others to. And you, Grady, just you wait till Papa gets ahold of your hide."

From behind them a soft voice said, "After me, your papa comes first."

Ole Raggey stood there, all two hundred and fifty pounds of ice, flicking that swagger stick across his hand. Folks said he'd been a hero in the war, and Bubba was sure he'd killed off those old Krauts with that same smile on his face.

Raggenbotham pulled his shirt cuffs down and rolled back his shoulders. "You gentlemen know we don't permit fighting in this schoolyard. Perhaps you forgot the rules?" He looked at Bubba.

"No sir," Bubba mumbled.

"What's that again? A little louder, Mr. Harkins. I didn't quite hear what you said."

"No sir," Bubba said louder, and swallowed. Across the quiet schoolyard, he saw Mr. Tetley watching from just inside the doorway.

"And you, Mr. Ferrell?" Grady shook his head, his handkerchief over his mouth. "Speak when you're spoken to, Mr. Ferrell!" Raggenbotham snapped. "And stand when I address you."

Grady pulled himself to his feet. He wiped the blood away with his sleeve and tried to say "No sir." But on the *s* he lisped, and a tooth flew out of his mouth. The children laughed.

"Quiet!"

They fell back to guarded silence. The sweat trickled down Bubba's back, stinging in the raw gravel cuts. He'd never seen Ole Raggey so mad.

"And you, young Harkins," the fat roll on Raggey's neck smoothed out as he looked down at Scooter. He slapped the stick against his knife-pleated trousers.

Bubba clenched his hands. Oh Lord, make Scoot behave, he prayed, for his brother had that cocky look and he didn't know yet about people like Ole Raggey.

"Let me make this clear," the teacher went on, "for no reason, I repeat, for *no* reason, are you to fight at this school. Respect for your betters and discipline are the key. I'm sure the inestimable Mrs. Ruby has mentioned such things?"

69

"Yes sir," Scooter replied, and from the look on his face, Bubba could tell he was trying to figure out what Ole Raggey had called his mama.

Raggenbotham held the cane parallel in both hands as he faced the two older boys. "Present your backs."

Reluctantly, Bubba turned, and so did Grady. Bubba braced himself, but the cane landed instead with a *thunk* on Grady's back. *Swoosh!* Again the *thunk*, harder, and the boy let go a grunt.

Two hits. Goshamighty, Ole Raggey must be some mad. Ole Raggey could raise a welt. Good for Grady for not yellin'. Now Bubba braced himself for his turn and bit down hard. He'd been smacked before, seemed like Raggey had it in for him sometimes, but he'd never given him the satisfaction of crying out. The cinders crunched.

Whoosh! Thunk! And this time Grady did cry out. Two more times it came, Bubba bracing himself each time, but Grady receiving the blow, until finally the boy went on his knees, sobbing, and Bubba saw the blood seeping into the back of his shirt.

"Enough, Mr. Ferrell?"

"Yes sir, Mr. Raggenbotham sir," Grady babbled, his handkerchief wedged in his eyes.

Bubba felt a wash of pity. Behind him, he heard Raggey move, and knew it was his turn. He straightened his shoulders and closed his eyes. Again the cane swished, but a scream split the air. Bubba whirled around. Scooter was holding onto Raggey's arm, the blood beading on a red ridge across his face. He must have run up to defend him and taken the blow. Raggenbotham shook him off. "Get away from me, boy!"

Scooter brought his chin up. "You ain't gone beat my brother like that. I don't care who you are!"

"We'll just see about that, young man. Mr. Tetley, please escort this insubordinate child inside while I deal with his brother."

Tetley's face was so pale as he hurried across the yard that Bubba felt sorry for him. The teacher put his arm around Scooter, but the boy pulled back. "And don't you go calling me no names, neither!" he yelled.

Raggenbotham pulled down his sleeves with a snap. "Enough!"

A vein stood out blue in Raggey's neck, and with a flash of hate, Bubba wished it would pop. "Go on inside, Scoot," he said, and Tetley hustled the reluctant boy away. He made sure his brother was well inside the schoolhouse, then turned and squared his shoulders once more.

Footsteps crunched close behind him on the gravel. "Let us learn discipline now, Mr. Harkins. Once and for all, let us learn discipline." The steps moved back. When they stopped, Bubba bit his lip again and concentrated on the metallic taste of his own dried blood, and waited for the blows to come.

8

For Bubba, each step on the walk home hurt from his bones out. He held his body steady, willing himself not to cry. Scooter was staying close, the welt on his face red with Mr. Tetley's iodine, and it wouldn't do for the boy to see him break down, but he sure would be glad to get home. Usually Scoot was all over the place, either zigzagging his way across the road from one ridge to the other that the scraper had pushed up, or scrambling down a ditch bank. Today he wasn't paying any attention to the water lilies blooming in the ditch, nor even to the dust swirls in the road where a snake had slithered across. Scoot just stuck beside him, his eyes worried. Finally he asked, "You hurtin' bad?"

"Not too bad," Bubba lied.

Relief washed over Scooter's face. "Does that old man always beat kids like that?"

"Naw. He usually quits after a lick or two."

"I'm glad I got Mr. Tetley for a teacher. I don't want to grow up and have Ole Raggey."

"Now don't you start into callin' him that." Bubba ran his tongue over his lips. It hurt to talk. "To you, he's Mr. Raggenbotham. You start thinkin' different, you liable to say it to his face."

"We sure taught them boys not to pick on us."

Bubba tried to grin. "Didn't know you was part dog. Queen would be proud."

They walked past a field of tobacco yellowing as it ripened in the sun. Bubba held his breath against the peppery smell to keep from sneezing. The pain pulled across his back as he stumbled and righted himself. When he finally saw the chinaberry tree, it shimmered and he dared not blink. Queen bounded across the yard with a sharp bark, her tail circling in joy. Suddenly she stopped, her nose quivering. She circled the boys, smelling their overalls, then she looked up at Bubba with a low whimper. He knelt stiffly, his throat tight, and put his arm around the black shaggy neck. "It's all right, girl," he said, and wiped his eyes on her coat before Scooter could see.

"What you all doin' home so early?" Ruby's voice came from the porch. "Lordamercy, what the world has happened to you boys?"

"Lordamercy, Bubba!" his mama said again. She had unbuttoned his overall straps and was trying to take off his shirt, but it had stuck to his back. "Hold on a minute," she said as she hurried to the stove.

Bubba was bent over the table, surrounded by the turpentine smell of Astyptodyne lotion she'd used to clean his face. Scooter sat beside him, his eyes riveted on his brother's back.

A warm smoothness soaked through Bubba's shirt as Ruby's gentle hands rubbed melted lard in to ease the fabric free. He bit his lip as the dried blood pulled away. She sucked in her breath. "Oh, Bubba," she whispered. He hadn't cried in front of his mama since his daddy went away, but he knew if he saw her face, he would now. He traced the fruit pattern on the oilcloth with his fingernail and braced himself for the questions he knew were coming. Her hand fell lightly on his head. "Son, Oscar Raggenbotham done this to you?" Bubba nodded. "Over a schoolyard fight?"

"I guess he felt he had to set an example and all. It ain't so bad."

She stopped filling the basin with warm water from the stove reservoir and turned, angry. "It's bad enough, boy! And I don't want to hear no more excuses for him out of you!" The water slopped over as she put the basin on the table, but she didn't notice. Her eyes were on his back again. "How many times he hit you?"

"Five."

"Five! With that stick of his?" He nodded. She touched the welts again with hands so light he could hardly feel them. "Broke the skin. Must've hurt bad."

"Yes'm. But I didn't let on."

"I wish you'd hollered to high heaven," she said.

"Maybe give the folks around here somethin' to think on. Hurt my boys like this, he deserves a whipping. Ain't like it's the first time he's used that stick."

"He's the meanest man I ever saw," Scooter said with a decisive nod. "How come he's so mean?"

"His family was all like that."

"Seems like he wouldn't go around beatin' on people then. Seems like he'd know better," Bubba said.

"Feels natural, I reckon. That temper will be his undoing one day." She started cleaning his back. The soap seared so, Bubba put his teeth against his arm to not cry out. When the rag splashed in the enamel bowl, he saw it leave the water pink. He looked away quick at the sight of the tears standing in his mama's eyes.

Sorry Grady Ferrell. Sorry Jarvis Badden. Sorry Oscar Raggenbotham. Sorry Jed Harkins. There, he'd said it. Sorry Jed Harkins. Hadn't been for him, he wouldn't have had no need to fight, no need for his mama to doctor his back, no need for her to cry. He wished his father had never come home.

"Of course, Oscar's mama wont that way," Ruby went on quickly, as if to keep her mind off what she was doing, "she was a fine person. I'll have to say he was good to her while she lived. That's why he started buyin' land, a place for her. He don't have nothin' to do with the rest of his family."

Maybe they don't want to have nothin' to do with

him, Bubba thought as she tossed the water out the back door and pumped fresh into the basin.

She was rinsing his back when footsteps sounded on the porch and the door clicked open. Bubba tried to sit up, but Ruby's hand held firm. "You stay right there till I'm done."

Jed came in. "What the devil?"

"Scooter," Ruby said quickly, "go fetch me that red jar of salve off my dresser." The boy hesitated.

"You heard your mama. Run on now, son." Jed eased him out the door. Then he turned back, his face grim.

"I had to grease his shirt to get it off," Ruby said, her voice sharp in the still room.

"Oscar Raggenbotham?" Jed's voice was quiet. She nodded. Bubba felt his father's hand touch his neck. "You all right, boy?"

Bubba kept his head down. "Yes sir."

"Those marks are pure ridges, Jed. Our boy's gone bear scars the rest of his life."

His father's hands felt surprisingly soft, in spite of the new raised calluses. "I see it, Ruby."

Scooter came back in. "This the right jar, Mama?"

"Fine," she nodded. The remembered smell made Bubba's eyes sting. Camphor, dried roses, peat, vinegar, and the sweet smell of honey: one of Lily's concoctions. The medicine felt cool as Ruby smoothed it on.

"All right, tell me what happened," Jed said.

"It wont our fault, Daddy," Scooter said. "Really. Some boy was shooting off his mouth at Bubba, and Bubba hit him. Then another boy tried to get in it, and that wont fair, so I bit him good." He grinned. "We beat the daylights out of 'em. But then Ole Raggey hit Bubba and that other boy for fightin', and I got hit, too, but it was a mistake. And we got sent home early, and are you and Mama mad?" he finished, the words tumbling out in a rush.

"No, son, we're not mad," Jed said. "Matter of fact, I'm right proud. I didn't know I had me two fightin' Harkinses. Bubba used to windmill his arms around some, but looks like he's growed up to take care of hisself, and you, too." He looked at Bubba, but Bubba just held still.

Scooter sat and slid his arm around his brother's waist and whispered, "I wish I'da bit Ole Raggey, too. I'd bite him right now if'n I had the chance."

"I know. You tried to stop him," Bubba answered.

"You reckon I'll have me a scar, too?"

"Little pitchers have big ears," Ruby said.

"I wont eavesdroppin', I just heard. I hope I do get a scar, just like Bubba's and Daddy's."

Bubba blinked. He'd all but forgotten about the scars on his father's back. Gray, ropy things.

Ruby said, "Scooter, you're next. Get undressed."

"Aw, Mama, Mr. Tetley already doctored me with that stingin' old iodine," he whined.

"You do what your mama says, boy," Jed snapped.

With his lip stuck out, Scooter peeled off his shirt and overalls, his white skin shining in the dim kitchen. The red scrapes stood out sharp. Jed looked away, his fists tight. "Man ain't got no right beatin' my boys like that," he muttered.

Scooter heard him. "Aw, these ain't from Ole Raggey, Daddy. The kids just played a trick on me. We were playin' jump rope, see, and they were going "Jailbird, jailbird," and when they got to the part about the guard closing the gate, they pulled the rope tight and I fell down, and that's when Bubba . . ." His voice trailed off, and Bubba could see the knowing coming behind his eyes as he looked at his father. His hand came up to his mouth and he said simply, "Oh."

Jed sighed. "I see. So that's the way it was. Mighty obliged to you, Bubba."

"Wont nothin'. Mama taught us to stand up for our own, and I was standin' up for Scooter."

Jed's eyelids dropped, and he looked away, nodding. "Only right you should. Scooter's a lucky boy to have a brother like you." He turned and left the room, the slap of the screen loud in the silence he left behind.

9

Bubba cut across the field, careful to avoid the sharp stubble. Beyond the neat rows of haystacks, the October woods blazed scarlet and gold. A covey of quail lifted on startled wings, their whir and wind surrounding him. He watched them pepper the intense blue sky, wishing he'd brought his gun, but he'd had other things on his mind. Yesterday he'd watched Scoot limp home from school in those ill-fitting brogans and seen him peel the wool socks down from his oozing blisters, and he'd decided to face it out with Israel about doing some trapping. Furs brought in good money, and he couldn't keep saying Bubba was too young forever.

A thin stream of smoke drifted from the Wades' chimney. Lily's gourds hung ripe on the fence, and her yellow garden mums were bright against the ruffled green collards. She was at the clothesline, dropping her clean clothes in stiffened peaks into her basket. He found Israel at the corncrib, shucking dried corn.

"Hey boy, what you doin' here this time of day?"

"Wanted to talk to you about somethin'."

Israel grinned. "Glad to see you. Reckon those hands of yourn can work same time as your mouth?"

"Reckon so." Bubba sat beside him and pulled back the dry husk on an ear of corn. He ran a corncob up the hard kernels to pop them off. "Wondering could you teach me to use them traps."

"What about them rabbit boxes we made last year?"

"I been usin' them. Thing is, I'm after pelts what can make me some good money."

"You talkin' muskrat and otter?" Bubba nodded. "You don't want much, do you, boy? Them animals is few and far between — that's how come their pelts is so dear. And you talkin' bout using a steel trap."

"I know. But you said last year that I might be old enough to use one this year."

Israel rolled his eyes. "Throwin' my own words back in my mouth." Shifting his rump on the bench, he packed his homemade pipe, lit it with a kitchen match from his pocket, then pinched out the flame. He puffed, then: "You talkin' special money, seems to me."

"Shoe money."

He looked down at Bubba's dusty feet and chuckled. "Reckon they have growed some."

Bubba tucked his feet farther under the bench. "Scooter needs shoes, too. Them hand-me-downs are tearin' up his feet. Bad enough for him at school as it is."

Israel looked at him. "More trouble?"

Bubba studied the corncob. "I don't know. Scooter ain't talkin'. No tellin' what them kids doin'."

Israel's eyes were sympathetic. "How your back?"

"Healed up, 'cept for the itchin'."

"Let me see." When he pulled his shirt up, Israel let out a soft "Uh *huh*. You and your daddy sure gone just about match." He caught Bubba's look and added, "Course, your scars ain't dirty-lookin' like his. Yours gone blend right in." He tilted his head. "You know how your daddy come by them scars, don't you?"

Bubba looked away. "In prison, I guess."

"No sirree!" Israel said. "He come by them scars same way you did." At Bubba's surprised look, he nodded, "That's a fact. That Oscar Raggenbotham, it his first year teachin' here, and Mist Jed's last year at school. Those two crossed hairs right from the beginnin' — your daddy was natcherly high-spirited, and Ole Raggey, he want everybody to toe the line — and by Christmastime, both they tempers was short. One day, Mist Jed was cuttin' up some in class, and way I hear tell it, that there teacher just flew into a hot temper and started strikin' out with that stick of his'n, and Mist Jed tryin' to get away, and 'fore he knew it, Ole Raggey whopped that stovepipe flyin'," Israel's arm swung so hard he almost hit Bubba, "and soot went everywheres, and him still just a beatin' on Mist Jed."

Israel knocked his pipe against the bench. Bubba's hands were still, his eyes waiting. "That is, till some of

81

the other big boys — Shade Fields and Ray Foster — grabbed that stick right outten his hand, then took Mist Jed on home. Mist Hugh — your grandaddy — so fit to be tied, he go over to that school and get Mist Jed's things and say his boy ain't goin' back there again. That's how come your daddy never finished school. Mist Hugh and Miss Lonie raised such a fuss, everybody got riled." Israel shook his head. "Maddest I ever seen Ole Raggey, him bein' shamed like that. He almost lost his job, but for Miss Virginia. She was well thought of, and here her boy had just come back from the war, and he a hero, so they gave him another chanct. But he ain't never forgive your daddy for that shamin'." Israel stopped for breath. "Your daddy still carryin' that soot around, and that man still carryin' his spite. Could be you got a taste of that."

"But my daddy let him get away with beatin' us."

Israel picked up another cob. "Maybe your daddy figures least said is soonest mended. Ain't easy for him to stand by, but that what he think best. You goin' on to high school next year, but Scooter gone be there a long time. And that teacher is one grudge-bearin' man. Mist Jed shame him, he gone get meaner. And the way things is now, most folks ain't too inclined to stand behind your daddy." Bubba looked down, embarrassed. Israel put his big hand on his shoulder. "Time gone change that, boy. Peoples is gone realize he the same fine man he always been. But now ain't the time to stir up ill feelin's his boys'd have to pay for. Them scars on Ole Raggey's brain just as much as they on Mist Jed's back. Best you have a care."

Bubba nodded. Maybe sharing scars with his daddy wont so bad. "I'll watch out for Scooter, too."

"See that you do," Israel nodded. "Reckon it wouldn't hurt for you to holp your daddy out some," he said. "You certain you can handle one of them traps?"

"Sure, if you show me how."

"Huh, I sure ain't gone lend you one any other way." Israel pushed himself to his feet. "Let's us see if you man enough to set one." Bubba dropped his corn-cob and jumped up. Guinea hens skittered ahead of Israel's long legs and dashed pell-mell into the bushes. Bubba hurried along, taking two steps to Israel's one.

In the sudden shade of the barn, he blinked to accustom his eyes as Israel pulled a trap out from the straw, saying, "Ain't even got 'em out yet, too early to trap much." The steel trap gleamed with last year's oiling, the sharp zigzag teeth catching the light. Israel wiped it with a rag, then pressed the lever. "This how you open it. You gone need to do it with your foot — I doubt your arm's strong enough yet." Bubba looked at the open jaws of the wicked-looking trap and figured using his foot would be just fine. "Now this the tricky part," Israel went on. "You gone have to reach with your hand to set it so it'll stay open. You be careful and handle it double careful when you placin' it." He had Bubba practice and finally said, "I think you got it now." He narrowed his eyes. "You gone take care usin' this thing, boy?"

"I got no urge to lose a hand."

Israel nodded. "And best to leave Miss Queen home. She not spry as she was, and them muskrats, they'll jump what get close, trap or no trap." Over Bubba's protest, he said, "You smart, you listen and do what I say."

Lily's voice called, "Israel, Mist Jed's here."

"Come back over in the mornin'," Israel said as he left the barn. "I want to holp you set it the first time." Bubba shoved the trap back under the straw, his mind full of rich furs, and people admiring, and all the things he could buy his mama.

When he came out into the sunlight, he saw his father talking to Israel with a wide grin on his face. "I got me a job picking cotton at the Hopkins place," he was saying. He looked surprised when he saw Bubba. "What you doin' over here, boy?"

"He been holpin' me while we been havin' us some man talk," Israel said.

Jed's eyes flickered. "That's fine. I'm glad he's willin' to help. But from now on, Bubba, you let your mama know where you off to." He looked at Israel. "Half the time we don't know where he's at," he explained with a shrug.

"Well, he kinda used to goin' and comin' as he pleases," Israel said softly.

Bubba's ears stung. He didn't like being corrected in front of Israel. And there was Lily in hearing distance, too. He walked away, not hearing Israel's "See you in the mornin' " nor Lily's soft "Bye."

10

Bubba had just gotten home and started chopping wood out back when he saw his father striding up the path with a face like thunder. Ruby came to the screen door, but when Jed stepped across the breezeway and headed for him without speaking to her, Bubba felt his new-healed scars start to itch like a fire was in them.

"Bubba, you got no business hangin' round Israel's all the time," Jed said. "Your mama needs you here for chores. She can't spend all her time chasin' you down."

Bubba's chin came up. "I get my chores done."

"Don't give me no backtalk. Seems like you're over there more than here."

Ruby stepped out the door into the tension, her eyes flicking from one to the other as she brushed flour from her hands. For some reason, she made Bubba think of a mama bird dragging her wings in the dust to take attention away from her babies. "He and Israel always been close," she said.

"Huh, more'n likely worryin' him to death. Israel got better things to do than baby-sit." Bubba's face flared. "Best not be taking advantage. Understand?"

He only muttered "Yes sir" because he felt his mama's eyes on him. They went inside and left him to finish chopping the wood.

Baby-sittin'! Jed Harkins didn't have no call saying that. *I wont never a baby since the day he left. Me and Israel are friends, we been through a lot.* His mind burning, Bubba struck the ax down with a vengeance on a piece of wood, letting splinters fly, not even noticing the pungent piney smell. *That ole man don't know nothin' bout those years skimpin' by.*

The ax kept rhythm with his thoughts. What did *he* know about bein' down to just a few chickens, and corn shrivelin' and the precious seed all used? Or haulin' buckets of water to keep a few plants alive? About gatherin' branches 'cause he wasn't strong enough to haul wood by himself once the mules were gone?

He lowered the ax, catching his breath. Those mules now. Lightnin' sold to pay the taxes, and then Maypop . . . Jed Harkins shoulda been in the cornfield with them *that* day, it hot as blue blazes and the soda itchin' their arms, and Baby Scooter sittin' on the soda bags in the cart just a whinin', and Maypop wearin' his tail out flickin' flies away. Wont no breath of air to be had in those tight rows of cornstalks. The mule's sweaty coat had stood up in points, and Scooter's blond hair was damp curls, his face red as his mama's. Finally, Ruby had broadcast a last handful of soda along the yellowing stalks and said, "Best I get him back to the house. This heat ain't fit for chick nor child." She'd lifted the baby to her hip and left.

He'd worked until the sun was high, then undone the mule from the traces and swung up onto its slippery back. He kicked at Maypop's round sides with his bare heels as they circled the field for home. He pinched away some threads of a spiderweb caught in his eyelashes, and at that moment Maypop shied back.

A snake coiled in front of them, its tail shaking like dry beads. The mule flung up its head, then leveled into a run. Startled, Bubba tried to hang on. Maypop headed straight for the house, and there was Scooter playing in the yard. "Mama! Mama!" Bubba screamed, and as he started to slide, he saw her throw the tin washtub clanging down the porch steps to distract the maddened mule as she jumped, arms outstretched to shield the baby. But the clatter only panicked Maypop more, and Bubba thought surely they would run them down.

A low black streak ran out from under the porch, growling and snapping at Maypop's legs. The mule turned, and Bubba slid off into the dirt. Queen was in full cry as he ran past her to catch up with the mule galloping out of sight, its harness lines trailing. A scream spun up into the air. Bubba's stride broke, then he ducked his head and ran around the edge of the cornstalks.

The mule was on its side, eyes rolling, breath honking like a cry. Bone stuck out of its foreleg like a broken stick, and foamy slobber spattered its muzzle. Sickened, Bubba turned away and saw his mama come running, holding her skirts out of the way, the other hand flinging out and back. He stepped forward to block her view. He didn't want her to see, for she was tenderhearted.

"Let me by!"

"Won't do no good, Mama." She looked at him, her eyes wide. "He done broke his leg, and ain't nothin' you can do can help him." She started forward again, but he put his hand on her arm. "I said No, Mama." He turned her gently, his mind working fast. "You go on back to the house. I'll take care of everything."

"Lord God, Bubba, you ain't gone . . . ?"

"No ma'am, I'll go get Israel Wade."

A long look, and then she gave in to the new note of authority in his voice and went back to the house.

When Israel had looked at the suffering mule, he'd muttered, "Ain't no help for it," and raised his gun. Bubba heard the shot, even with his hands over his ears. Then he'd felt Israel's hand on his back, and he'd leaned into the comfort, the overalls stiff against his cheek.

And can't cut no land without a mule, so there had gone their last chance of making a living from the farm. And Jed Harkins hadn't been there to see the despair or hear his mama readin' the Bible every night about frettin' not and God's promise to send angels to bear them up. Which He did. He had sent Israel Wade.

Bubba raised the ax and smacked the wood. *Thwack!*

Jed Harkins hadn't seen her tying herself to the plow and bending to pull it while Bubba guided, and he hardly big enough to see over it. *Thwack!* And her too proud to ask for help, the lines cutting deeper in her face. Until the day Israel saw. He had walked up and undone the traces, saying quietly, "Ain't fittin' you should do that, Miss Ruby. Israel will take care. You go on now." And Bubba had wept to see her slump on the porch, her head on her arms, her shoulders heaving. And Israel had left and brought back Lily for comfort and his mules for work and seed for planting. *Thwack!* And Lily doctorin' them and watchin' Scooter while they worked. And Israel teaching him things so they got a little cash money from his huntin' and fishin'. He'd heard his mama praying many a time at night, "Thank you, Lord, thank you, for Israel and Lily Wade." *Thwack!* And them waitin' and prayin' for the day his daddy would come home and things would be right again. *Thwack!* And here they'd all been wrong. Ain't no good come out of him being home, Bubba thought. No good atall.

"You choppin' enough wood for the whole winter, boy?" Israel's voice came from the breezeway.

He stopped. He hadn't heard Israel come up. He looked, amazed at the amount of kindling that littered the yard. Panting, he gave Israel a sheepish grin. "Looks like it, don't it?"

"Well, you run out of wood here, there's plenty to my house. You can cut me some after we set that trap in the mornin'. Can always use some good help."

Jed came out on the porch and Bubba looked away, but the warm feeling Israel gave him stayed. Huh. Baby-sittin'. Ole Jed Harkins didn't know nothin'.

He woke impatient to be gone to Israel's, but his face fell as he came into the warm kitchen and saw the reed basket full of freshly ironed curtains. He glared at the mound of crisp ruffled lace. Such fancy stuff looked out of place in his mama's kitchen. His father didn't want her taking in Mrs. Fields's work either, but she said they needed the money and she didn't mind.

Now Jed gulped down the last of his coffee and pushed the bench back with a scrape.

"You going already?" Ruby asked.

"Sooner I get there, the heavier the cotton in my bag." He turned to Bubba. "Your mama got somethin' for you to do, and then you best fix that hogpen today. Won't do to have 'em get out."

Bubba nodded, his disappointment sharp. He looked up just as Jed opened the door and saw him glance at the wash basket. His father's face hardened, and he closed the door behind him with a snap.

Ruby cleared her throat. "Guess you figured out by now them curtains needs to be taken to Mrs. Fields." His mouth full of eggs, Bubba nodded. Maybe if he hurried, he could still get to Israel's today. "Sure hope they suit her," Ruby said, fingering the delicate lace before throwing a cloth over the top. "You be careful carryin' them things. You know how she is."

He knew. Mrs. Fields always made him feel like his ears needed to be washed or something.

Bubba slid the basket onto the Fieldses' porch and knocked while Queen waited patiently on the road. The gleaming brass doorknob turned, and Mrs. Fields stood there, her eyebrows raised. "Brought your washin', Mrs. Fields, from my mama." When she stepped to the basket and lifted each layer of curtains to peer at the next, he was indignant. His mama did good work — Mrs. Fields knew that. He wrinkled his nose at the dry, mediciney smell that came through the doorway.

From the corner of his eye he saw Mr. Fields crossing around the back of the house. He winked at Bubba but didn't say anything. Shade Fields usually didn't. He was a big, quiet man some said was tied to his wife's apron strings, but Bubba knew better. Many a time he had come by their house to leave a bushel of corn, or a pailful of peppers, and once even a ham. His mama had worried about taking charity from them, until one day he'd blurted, "Never you mind about payin' back. What them what doesn't know don't know won't hurt 'em, and we got enough and to spare." So she had smiled, and Mr. Fields had mumbled, "All right," and left. From that time on, Bubba had never wondered where the gifts on the porch came from, and he didn't mind taking from Shade Fields.

Mrs. Fields straightened up. "These will be fine." Her lips pulled back in an unaccustomed smile, and he suddenly remembered Tom Sly telling how she'd dropped her teeth in the horse trough once and stayed in bed a week from it. As if she read his mind, her smile vanished, and she went back inside, calling "Sha-ade!" as Bubba hurried away with the empty basket. Huh, he bet she wont gone find ole Shade to hang no curtains.

As he ran home, he pulled in deep breaths of the bright October air to clear his nose of the doctor smell, his resentment beating at him like the basket knocking against his leg. Queen loped ahead, running crooked as she looked back at him. When they came to the path to Israel's, he stopped. Wouldn't take long to fix that fence, and he did need to learn how to set that trap. Queen sat waiting, her tail swishing in the dust. When he swung off the road, she followed.

Israel saw him coming. "Bout give up on you, boy."

"Had to take Mrs. Fields her laundry."

Israel eyed his sullen face. "She get your goat?"

"She's so stuck-up, she makes me mad as fire."

"Unlax, boy. You gone let that woman ruin your whole day? You wont with her but just a few minutes."

"She ought not act like she does."

"She gone act like she gone act. Didn't you see that ingrown face?" He shook his head, "Tell you what, Bubba, folks ain't gone always behave the way you think they should. Sooner you learn that, sooner you'll save yourself a lot of grief." He smiled. "You learn to work that trap right, it save you a lot of grief, too."

"Ain't got much time. Got me a hogpen to fix 'fore Daddy gets home."

"Wouldn't do to have your daddy upset over no hogpen. I'll help."

At day's end, Bubba was tired but excited. At the creek, Israel had showed him how to look for slide marks where the muskrats' dens were, and made him practice setting the trap time and again. He'd said it wasn't cold enough to place it yet, but Bubba had left the trap set, just in case. They'd gotten the pen fixed, too.

When he came into the kitchen, Jed was holding his

hands out as Ruby smoothed ointment on his raw fingertips. Scooter was rocking a Mason jar of cream back and forth as he watched. The sight of the swollen hands shocked Bubba. His daddy's had never been that tender.

"You get that fence fixed?" Jed asked.

Bubba nodded. He avoided his father's eyes, suddenly remembering he'd been off with Israel and hadn't told his mama where he'd be.

"Them cotton bolls eat you up alive," Ruby fussed.

Jed grinned at her soft clucking. "What you takin' on so for? Hands'll get tough."

"You gone pick cotton again come Monday, Daddy?" Scooter asked. Jed nodded.

"Jed, you're surely not," she protested.

"These hands got all day tomorrow to heal, Ruby."

Pressing her lips shut, she turned to Scooter. "Go put this ointment away for me, son."

When he jumped up, the Mason jar rumbled across the floor. At Ruby's look he said, "It ain't broke, Mama. That jar ain't never gone make no butter anyway. I shook and shook."

"You shake some more when you get back. The butter'll come," she said. Making a face, he left.

Jed grinned. "Bet he won't be back for an hour."

But she looked hard at him. "Ain't no call you killin' yourself for some money. We been gettin' by."

"Gettin' by ain't enough. Need to get some seed money set by, and tax money."

"I don't like to see you hurtin'."

"And I ain't likin' to see you taking in Alma Fields' dirty wash."

Their eyes locked. Ruby dropped hers first.

Bubba surprised himself by saying, "I could go."

They looked at him. Jed's head pulled back. "You got school and aplenty to do around here."

"Scooter can help Mama."

"Scooter's too young to do much."

"Ain't no younger than I was when you went off."

Jed looked away. "Well, I thank God ain't no need for that now, not as long as I'm able. And it'll take more than two sore hands to put me down."

"Your daddy picked a hundred pounds today, Bubba," his mama said into the silence.

He blinked. A good man could pick two, three hundred pounds a day. He remembered how his daddy used to move down the rows, his hands flying and his eyes laughing as he made a game of the work.

"Out of practice slowed me up today," Jed said.

But Bubba didn't hear him. He was still thinking about his daddy that had gone away and this poor excuse of a man that had come back.

11

Bubba pulled his daddy's mackinaw coat closer against the cold November air. Vapor drifted from the white frosted fields as he heard a far crack of gunfire, then saw a spiral of smoke rise into the pearling sky from the marshes across the creek.

He didn't know why he was coming down here again. Israel had been right, too early to set that trap out. Been better off using a gun. He stuck his nose in his jacket to thaw his face. These cold mornings, he was glad of Jed's boots to protect his feet. The rutted path was gouged into sharp frozen clods from the logging sleds that had worked the woods that summer.

At first he'd gotten up every morning before the clock chimed and raced to check the trap. But as the days went by, he lost his hurry. Seemed like there weren't no muskrat to be had, though he'd placed the trap in the shallows of the creek anywhere he'd seen a likely hole for a muskrat's den.

Ahead, a blue heron stretched its long curved neck and cruised low over the water. The clay bank dropped sharply to the creek, and Bubba worked his way down the root-formed steps. Suddenly ducks scrambled into the air with a ruffle of wings, and he jumped back with a startled "Oh!" As he grabbed for a handhold, he saw a dark spot move among the reeds below. He crouched and crept farther down, his heart pounding a solid *thump thump*. The trap was partway out of the water, and a muskrat pulled this way and that, trying to free its leg. Israel's words came back: "That ole muskrat, he meaner'n a fox and twice as sly. Don't you go near him lest you mean business."

Bubba scrambled back up the bank and grabbed a big butt of a tree branch. When he got back, he saw the muskrat heaving and thrashing its slick black tail, bigger around than a man's thumb. He gripped the club and came closer. The animal's foot was caught in the trap, revealing the rich bluish gray undercoat. It saw him, and the small black eyes shone with a vicious yellow light, waiting for him to make a move. Bubba almost lost his nerve, but he looked again at the dark brown fur shining against its back and marveled at the muskrat's size. The thought of the money such a pelt would bring made his excitement swell. Swallowing, he hefted the branch over his head and stepped closer.

Suddenly, the muskrat darted forward, baring its sharp teeth. It shocked Bubba so, he shouted and brought the butt down hard, then struck again. He raised it once more, waiting. The body twitched, then lay still. Bubba lowered his trembling arms. The long groove from the branch stretched out deep in the mud on either side of the animal's head. Dead though it was, he could still see its eyes glowing with that hate. Stepping closer, he stroked the silky fur, but pulled away when he saw the bugs leaving the cooling body. Oh, it was gone be a pelt to be proud of!

As Bubba approached the house, Queen bounded up to meet him. Jed came out, his face stern. "You gone be late for school. Where you been?"

Queen sniffed around his back at the muskrat. "Trappin'," he said. His excitement broke through. "And I got me a muskrat. Lookahere!" He swung the animal forward, and Queen let out an excited bark.

"Trappin'! You too young to be trappin'."

"Naw I ain't. Just look," and he held the muskrat higher. Queen stretched her head up to sniff it.

"I see." But Jed didn't look, just called the dog back to his side. "What you been trappin' with?"

"Israel lent me one of his."

"Thought the man had better sense than to go giving a boy steel traps to play with."

"I wont playin'," Bubba said, hurt that his father hadn't even looked at his prize. "Israel taught me to use that trap careful-like. He knows I ain't no baby."

"Watch your mouth," Jed snapped. "Didn't I tell you to stay out from under his feet? No son of mine gone be trappin' till I've taught him myself. Israel best mind his own business, he knows what's good for him."

Bubba's jaw dropped. To say such about Israel! He threw down the muskrat and pulled off Jed's coat, then tore at the laces to get the boots off. The cold air striking his hot skin, he stared at Jed defiantly and headed stiff-legged for school. He felt his father watching him go, but he didn't care.

After school, Scooter's excitement over the fur eased Bubba's feelings. By the time he came out of the woods, the boy was already running ahead to the garden where Jed was burning leaves, his high voice carrying on the crisp air: "Daddy, Bubba says he caught him a muskrat! Can I see? Can I see?"

Jed looked over Scooter's head, across at Bubba. "It's over by the barn," he said, then threw another armful of leaves on the fire. Past the white smoke billowing up, Bubba saw Scoot run toward the pelt stretched out on a drying board propped against the barn wall. The wind shifted, and the smoke swept the ground, then lifted again as Jed said, "I went ahead and got it mounted. Don't want to wait to do somethin' like that." Bubba nodded. After a minute, Jed bent back to his work. In the distance, Scooter was smoothing his hand across the fur. Bubba headed toward the house instead.

The chinaberry tree looked like it had been strung with gold beads. Only a few leaves held on among the clustered berries, but the branches still intertwined to form a seat and give the illusion of shelter. Tempted, Bubba looked back, then shinnied up the tree to think. He worked his way up toward his favorite spot, the crook between the trunk and the biggest high branch, and leaned into its breast with a sigh. The branch cut into his rear, and he shifted, making the berries dance. When he was little, the seat had felt so big he'd had to hold on with both hands for fear of falling. It felt smaller now, but the scrape of the rough bark against his cheek was like an old friend. His eyes suddenly filled, blurring the landscape he'd known since he could first manage to climb so high. He blinked, and there was the house with its tin shake roof, and the cistern, then the henhouse and barn. Behind the graying smoke, he saw the grinding stone for sugar cane and the smokehouse where they hung hams to cure. Beyond where he could see were the hogpen and outhouse. Surrounding it all were the fields, and behind the border of trees he saw the rising smoke line from Israel and Lily's chimney like a friendly wave across the November air.

As he came into the kitchen that night, he overheard his parents talking softly. "Boy can't seem to understand I'm scared he'll get hurt," Jed was saying.

"Time'll come he will," Ruby assured him.

"Seemed all I could think about at prison was

comin' home and tellin' you all how much you mean to me, and here all I can do is shoot off my mouth." He gave her a twisted smile. "Some contrary man, do what I don't want and can't do what I do want."

They hushed when they saw him. Bubba ate what he could, but the food wedged halfway down. All he tasted was his disappointment. You'd think a man would have somethin' to say bout his son trapping such a fine muskrat. Israel would have.

12

The clock chimed six as Bubba yanked his half of the covers back from Scooter's curled-up body. The windows showed a graying sky, and he was glad it was Saturday. He pulled the quilt up around his ears.

Then he heard it again: footsteps coming up the steep attic stairs. His father crossed the room and shook Bubba's arm, laying his finger over his lips when he saw he was awake. "Come on," Jed whispered, and headed back down the stairs. Puzzled, Bubba got out of the warm bed, flinching at the cold floor. Quickly he pulled his overalls on over his long wool underdrawers and shirt. Wonder what the old man was up to? He'd made such a point of not waking Scooter up. The boy lay sound asleep, a fistful of quilt under his chin. Bubba pushed the covers up to his back and went downstairs.

Outside, heavy frost whitened the grass. Queen stuck her nose out from her hidey-hole as he hurried across the cold porch and into the warm kitchen.

A big breakfast was already laid out on the table. "Sit down and eat," Jed said, blowing on the coffee in his saucer. "We got business to take care of today."

His mama still hadn't said good morning. Bubba noticed how her eyes would slue around to Jed, like she wanted to say something, but wasn't sure how. More puzzled than ever, Bubba asked him, "What we gone do?"

"We're goin' to town. Get your stomach full, son. We got us a long walk ahead."

"Jed, don't you reckon Israel would . . . ?"

"We don't need Israel along, Ruby. This is Bubba and me business. This boy's got him a muskrat pelt to sell, and the fur man's gone be at the store today."

Goin' to sell his pelt? He'd been watching it cure, secretly pleased how it was turning out. There wont even a tear in the head where he'd bashed it.

"I just meant I'm sure Israel would be glad to ride you," Ruby said. "It's mighty cold to be walkin'."

"Don't need no more favors from Israel. We can walk it, right, Bubba?"

"Yes sir," he said, excitement sending his blood rushing. Goin' to sell his first fur!

The overcast sky had lifted by the time they reached the edge of town. With Jed's boots on, Bubba hadn't fared too badly in the cold. His tweed-billed cap kept his head warm, but his ears ached. The five miles had never seemed so long before, but on the way Jed agreed to let him deal for the pelt, and Bubba was pleased. He tucked his hands in his armpits to warm them, grinning at the rustle of the waxed paper he'd wrapped the pelt in before he'd stuck it down the front of his overalls.

A line of trucks and wagons were parked outside the store, and Bubba knew it would be crowded inside with people come to town to do their Saturday shopping, plus all the regulars that sat around the stove and talked, shooting long streams of tobacco juice at the carefully placed spittoons and missing more often than not. And the fur buyer would bring in even more trade.

The warmth hit them full in the face as they stepped in the door, and the familiar smells of tobacco, pickle juice, and kerosene filled Bubba's nose. The store had always been one of his favorite places. During the wintertime when his mama and Lily would come to town, he had spent most of his time here hunkered down in a corner, listening to the men's stories. For sure, the store regulars would admire his fine pelt.

Jed pushed the door closed behind them, and a silence fell across the room. Bubba saw the sly glances of the men, and his ears reddened. Across the room, Mrs. Fields stared, still holding a drape of fabric in her hand. When she deliberately turned her shoulder and sniffed, Bubba shrugged. Well, Israel was right, couldn't expect no better from her.

Henry Howell balanced his chair on its rear legs and shot a stream of tobacco juice into the spittoon, its *splat* loud in the silence.

"Got it that time, Henry," Tom Sly said, and the rest laughed.

"Hey Bubba." Thora had slipped away from the candy counter and come up to them. "Cold, ain't it?" She dug her hands down into her sweater pockets.

"Yeah." His tongue felt outsized. Behind him Jed cleared his throat, so he said, ears redder than ever, "This here's my daddy, Thora."

She stuck out her hand and grinned. "Hey there, Mr. Harkins. Sure have heard a lot about you."

A snicker came from the counter. Grady and Jarvis. Jed shook her hand. "Mighty pleased, Miss Thora."

Bubba saw people trying to hold back their grins and was relieved when Mr. Charles came over.

"You got some business here, Jed?"

"Monkey business, maybe," Henry muttered.

"Naw — he done left his shadow home," Little Joe

Sawyer said, and the men sniggered, watching Jed out of the sides of their eyes. Bubba knew they meant Israel.

So did Jed, for his head came up. "Bubba here's got somethin' he's lookin' to sell," he said.

Like a wind shifting, Charles smiled at Bubba the same friendly way he always had. "What you got, boy?" His smile made Bubba feel like he was being disloyal, and suddenly he wanted it over so they could leave. Then he saw Shade Fields wink, and felt better.

"Bubba's business is with the fur buyer," Jed said. "Show him, son."

"Did I hear someone inquire for a buyer?" The biggest fat man Bubba had ever seen rolled his way across the store. He was at least half a foot taller than Israel and so wide his arms couldn't lay flat at his sides. His shirt collar pinched his neck, and his cheeks glistened as he extended a white hand to Jed. "Flyer's my name, buying's my game. Glad to meetcha." As he pumped Jed's hand, his bay rum smell fanned out, leaving a bad taste in Bubba's mouth.

"Jed Harkins." Jed indicated Bubba, "But this here's the person you need to see."

"Ah. Harkins is the name, but the son plays the game." Flyer didn't appear to notice no one laughed with him. "What you got there, son? Somethin' you shot with your trusty gun?"

Grady snorted. Silent, Bubba pulled out the fur.

Flyer unfolded the waxed paper. "Muskrat, eh?" He ruffled the fur with his manicured hands, smoothed it, then flipped it over to examine the skin. "Nice cure. Nice fur. Reckon I could go fifty cents." He grinned, "That suit you, son? Pretty good for just trapping an animal and nailin' him on a board for a few days."

"No sir. I figure that pelt's worth more'n that."

Flyer's eyes widened. "More than fifty cents? That'd buy enough candy to make you feel dandy." The smile he flashed looked fake to Bubba. And seemed like he was poking fun, with that rhyming and all. His stubbornness rose. He thought of all the cold mornings he'd gone to check that trap, all the hoping, all the pride he'd felt. He took a deep breath and stood tall as he could. "I ain't after no candy, mister. I figure a prime fur like that ought to bring at least a dollar."

"A dollar? Good goshamighty!" Flyer appealed to his audience, for now everyone was watching. "You all hear that? This here boy thinks this pelt made out of gold. Son, the good Lord says not to be greedy."

"That's right," Bubba looked him in the eye, "and I hear He don't hold with stealin', neither."

Flyer's cheeks mottled pink. The men around the stove laughed, and Shade Fields said, "All right."

Bubba went on, "Mister, I worked a many a cold hour trappin' this muskrat. The Lord says a laborer is worthy of his hire, so I figure He'll find me another buyer if you won't give me a fair price."

"Amen," came Fields's voice, louder this time.

"Seventy-five," said Flyer.

Bubba shook his head. "No sir. I ain't gone take no less than this fine pelt's worth."

The buyer threw up his hands. "Boy, you sure you ain't got no Jew in you?"

He wasn't sure what Flyer meant, but he didn't like the way he said it. "No sir," Bubba answered, "not that I know of. Us Harkinses is good Christians."

"Yeah, ole Jed Harkins can turn water into wine," someone said, and the men laughed. Bubba's face flared.

Flyer's hand signaled surrender. "All right. A dollar asked, a dollar sold. I've bought a pelt worth its weight in gold."

Bubba shot a triumphant grin at his father, and across the room saw Shade Fields smiling ear to ear.

As Flyer handed Bubba a silver dollar, Charles picked up the fur. "Nice job of curing, Bubba."

"My daddy done it."

The storekeeper nodded, but his face shut down again. Grady and Jarvis came over for a closer look, and Bubba could see the reluctant admiration in their eyes.

Thora smoothed her hand across the pelt. "It's so soft. But he sure was a big one. Wont you scared?"

"Naw," he bluffed, pocketing the money. He felt Jed's look, and there in front of him were Thora's wide eyes. The truth pulled at him, and he remembered all that talk about being a Christian, so he said, "Well, maybe a little. But I was the one had the club."

The men laughed. "That's right, boy," Howell said. "Know for a fact how ornery them critters can get."

Charles said, "All that bargainin's thirsty work, boy. Bet you could stand a swallow of Co-Cola."

"Sounds like a fine idea. Make it two, Charles." Jed pulled two nickels out of his pocket. "Reckon I got bout dry as he did, waitin' to see how he'd do."

The liquid felt cold and sweet going down Bubba's throat. Now that the bargaining was all over, his knees threatened to shake, and he was glad when the men returned to their talk.

Henry Howell tilted his chair back again. "Hear tell that radio show other night bout scared ever'body to death."

Little Joe rolled his eyes. "Uh huh. Ilene took fright so bad, she went screamin' out in the road. Like to never got her back in the house."

"What you talk, Little Joe?" Howell laughed. "Heard when she run out that front door, you high-tailed it out the back, and wont till next mornin' she got you to leave that outhouse."

The men chuckled as Sawyer turned red. "Ain't nothin' to joke about," he mumbled. "Sounded so real."

"What color you reckon them Martians be?"

"Don't care, long as they ain't black. Got enough of them already," Leroy Cole said.

As the laughter rumbled around the stove, Bubba looked away. Sometimes it made him mad as fire to hear their talk. He was glad Israel wasn't there to hear it. Across the room, one of the men started talking to his father in a friendly fashion. Bubba went to join them, but shied back when he saw it was Ellis Mooney.

"You gettin' your place back in shape?" Mooney asked. Jed nodded. "Gettin' *all* your work caught up?"

"What you mean?"

"You know." Mooney's voice dropped. "Your stuff."

Jed stiffened. "I ain't making no stuff."

"Now, Jed. I understand once burned, twice shy. But I figure you got to have a few snorts tucked back. I might be willin' to take some of it off your hands."

"I ain't got nothin' tucked back."

"Aw now."

"Nothin'." Just that, cold and firm.

"Sure, sure. Just thought I'd ask, friendly-like." His eyes turned cold, "But maybe some folks don't need friends. White ones, that is." He walked away.

Jed's shoulders dropped, and then he saw Bubba. His head moved back as if to ward off a blow, then he said, "You ready to do some buyin' now, son?"

"We already got us a Co-Cola," Bubba said.

"I'm talkin' 'bout gettin' you some new shoes." When he didn't say anything, Jed put a hand on his shoulder and lowered his voice, "Israel told me you raisin' shoe money. Time for you to know, Bubba, you and me are the men of the house, and we need to talk

109

man to man sometimes. You and me, not you and Israel."

"He's my friend," Bubba said.

"He's my friend, too. But he's not your daddy, and we're not his family. He got enough to do to look out for his own. You understand what I'm sayin'?"

Bubba's lips pressed together. "I guess so." Now he felt bad about burdening Israel with their troubles.

"All right then. Now let's see about them shoes."

"Scooter's the one needs new shoes."

"He's got your old ones. You the one needs 'em."

He didn't want any shoes — that pelt money was Scooter shoe money. He remembered something and grabbed on to it. "Can't get no shoes today. All I got is this here dollar."

"For pity's sake, Bubba, you don't think I brought you off without bringing some money?" Jed blew out his breath. "Now, let's see what Charles has got, and I don't want to hear another word out of you."

Reluctantly, he followed his father back to the dry goods, ashamed for Mr. Charles to see his oversized boots. As he passed the men around the stove, Fields leaned back and said, "Nice pelt." Bubba nodded, and hoped they weren't looking at his feet.

As they walked home, the new shoes clunked against Bubba's back from their tied shoelaces. He'd put the boots back on, feeling it wouldn't be fair to Scooter to wear the new ones.

110

Jed was pleased with himself. "Figured I'd have enough to get you a decent pair of brogans. Looks like prison money spends as good as any other kind." When Bubba didn't answer, Jed grabbed his arm. "Hold on a minute there. Ain't you proud of them new shoes?"

"Be prouder they weren't bought with prison money."

"I worked hard for that money."

Bubba looked away from the hurt in his eyes. "Thought that money was for seed. We got to have that."

"Daddemmit, boy, you act like ain't no more ever comin' in! We got till spring to roust up seed money. Your need for shoes is now." He shook Bubba's shoulder. "Don't you be turnin' into no worrywart."

"Somebody better," Bubba muttered.

Jed's hand tightened. "Let's us get one thing straight, right now," he said. "I know you had a lot on you while I was gone, but I've about reached the end of my rope with your sass. Ain't your place to question what I do, or what I spend. I'll see to this family and its needs the best I can. You want to help out, fine, but you can forget about the worryin'. Worry don't get nothin' done, working does. I'll earn, and you'll earn, and we'll get by." He started walking again. After a minute, Bubba followed.

His father slowed until he caught up, then looked at him sideways. "Matter of fact, you might want to keep that silver dollar to put toward buyin' yourself a trap. Reckon you proved you big enough to handle one."

"Israel said I could use his."

"I took it back. Time we learned to look after ourselves, be a family again. I want us to stay away from them for a while."

Huh. It was mainly him over there most times, his father knew that. It didn't seem right for them to stay away from the Wades now, just 'cause they didn't need 'em. "You mean we can't be friends with them no more?"

"Listen, boy. Israel and me been friends from way back, but colored is colored, and white is white, and hangin' round them just makes things harder. Israel and me already talked about this, and he understands."

Bubba turned away, his eyes hot. Ain't no way Israel would ever understand, no more'n any other person would. Now he realized why Israel hadn't been over to the house lately, hadn't even come to see the muskrat skin. And why his mama had kept looking out the kitchen window, as if hoping for a sight of Lily coming down the path, her workbasket swinging over her arm.

Jed Harkins could talk friendship all day, but say what he would, he was just like the men at the store.

The new shoes weighed heavy on Bubba's shoulder as they walked down the road toward home.

13

The wire handle on the bucket cutting into his bare hand, Bubba crossed the yard under a lowering sky. His nose was running, and the cold wind knifed into his ears. Even the pigs were huddled together in a corner of the pen. "Soooee," he called, and dumped the slop bucket. The squealing pigs scrambled and butted each other to get to the trough. As he headed back, he saw the smoke whipping from Lily's chimney across the treetops, and the wanting to go there hit hard. He had sneaked over some, but sensed Israel holding back, and even Lily hadn't been the same. Once she'd almost touched him but stopped herself, and since then she'd kept her hands clasped together. The hurt in her eyes had hurt him, so he'd finally quit going.

Things just hadn't been the same without them. His mama quilted alone now with only the battery radio for company, and he missed hearing her and Lily laughing and sometimes singing together as they worked. They could sure make a pretty sound singing the old gospel hymns. Scooter was forever asking why they didn't come, and Bubba could tell Jed was grateful school

kept the boy distracted, for he had no answers that satisfied him.

Bubba pulled his collar up closer to his neck.
Above him the chinaberry tree branches crackled in
the wind, and more of the wrinkled gold berries littered the yard, joining the ones already clumped into
gooey yellow masses where they'd been stepped on.
The homeplace looked stark against the gray sky, the
only sign of life the smoke curling and blowing away
from the chimney. Gusts of wind whistled around the
corners, carrying the smell of woodsmoke on the air.
With its bare porch and tight-curtained windows, the
house looked closed in on itself, except for the
shimmer of light peeking through a curtain, like a
sliver of warmth to tease him back inside. As he
clunked the empty bucket down by the kitchen door,
the curtain pulled back. "Ain't you comin' in?" Ruby
called.

"In a minute. Got to chop some wood." He didn't
need to, but he was missing Israel somewhat bad right
now, and his mama could read him like a book.

Lifting the ax, he saw the broken pieces of pumpkin
next to the woodpile, all that was left of Thanksgiving.
Huh, it had been one sorry holiday without Israel and
Lily to laugh and share, like in past years. He could
still see Israel coming along the path like he used to,
with one of Lily's big hens slung across his back,
singing "Bringing In the Sheaves" at the top of his
lungs, and Lily carrying her basket full of fried apple

jacks, still hot. He and Scoot would run out in the cold to pick up pecans, then they'd crack nuts while the women cooked and Israel teased. Finally, the table would be loaded with food and the kitchen windows steamed up from all that cookin', and the room warm and bright against the cold outside.

Then Israel would say the blessing, always the same, his voice soft with respect: "Oh Lord, now here we are again to say a special thank-you for Your bounty. Bless these here families, Lord, them what's here and them what ain't," Bubba knew he meant Benjamin and Jed Harkins both, "And bless the land. And we pray You, Lord, us folks down here in the dark can find a way to walk in Your love and light. And we thanks You for these children, Lord, and asks You for patience, for You've dealt us somewhat a handful with these two."

And then he'd list all the food while the two boys squirmed: "Thank You, Lord, for these here turnips what you grew and Lily cooked, these here collards nurtured by Miss Ruby's hand . . ." and on and on until Scooter got tickled and Bubba's stomach rumbled. "Well, I'll hush now, Lord, for it sure would be a sin to encourage this here boy to go off giggling in Your presence. Amen and Amen." Laughing, they would heap their plates, faces shining in the lamplight. And Bubba realized he had never even noticed colored or white. All he had seen was people he loved. His daddy hadn't been there to see the ripening those years had brought, when Lily and Israel had become like their own blood kin, and now he'd changed that.

Who was going to keep the haunted look away from Lily's eyes now when she started missing Benjamin? Special holidays she missed her boy the most, but her pain seemed to fade when she saw Bubba and Scooter. He always tried to make her smile when he saw that look. It bothered him to think of the Wades eating alone and him not there to ease Lily's hurt.

The smell of fresh roasting coffee beans wafted from the house, and his mama came around the corner, a scarf wrapped round her head and her sweater front doubled tight under her arms. Wisps of hair blew around her face. "Land I pray, Bubba, you'll catch your death out here. I've got some fresh coffee just waitin' inside." He grinned. She knew how he loved coffee on a winter day. "Your daddy'll be in soon, and he might 'preciate a cup, too."

The cold wind hit the back of his neck, and he looked away. "In a minute. You go on."

"No dilly-dallyin', now." The wind whipped her skirt tight around her legs as she headed back.

She's hurtin' for some company, he suddenly realized. He split another piece of kindling. She ought not to have to do without the only friend she's got. I'm gone get this mess with Israel straightened out onct and for all. In his mind's eye, he saw Israel and Lily's chimney smoke again, like a hand beckoning him on. One man's say-so don't make friends quit being friends, he told himself. He knelt to load his arms with wood, his heart already lighter.

But come Christmas Eve, Bubba still hadn't talked with Israel. He'd gone over to their place twice, but it was almost like the man was avoiding him on purpose. He'd thought sure things would straighten themselves out, had even made a necklace for Lily out of chainey-ball seeds dyed with pokeberry juice and bought Israel a bright red handkerchief with his fishing money. The man did fair love red.

But things hadn't changed. Bubba poked the burning trash down and wiped his forehead. The warm day felt like spring, and as he headed to the house, he scratched at his long underwear where the sweat was making him itch. But the sun was starting to lower, and he knew it'd be cool soon enough.

Scooter was sweeping the yard, the dirt flying up in a cloud of dust. Chinaberries skittered ahead of the broom, rolling across the beaten dirt. He's gettin' dirty as sin, Bubba thought. Well, had to have a bath on Christmas Eve anyway.

Ruby came out on the porch, wrapped tight in her housecleaning apron. "For goodness sake, boy, how am I supposed to get this house clean, you stirrin' up all that dust and it comin' in every crack and cranny! You sweep this yard right, you hear? I want to see the brush marks, and not a single chaineyball waitin' to be stepped on and brought in this house."

Scooter stopped in midstroke. "But Mama, these ole berries don't even move if you don't hit 'em hard, this here broom is so wore out."

Ruby nodded. "Fine. When you finish up, get me some branches off that myrtle bush. Need a new broom for the new year anyhow."

"Aw, Mama," Scooter's face fell, "it's Christmas Eve. Ain't I gone get no time to play today?"

"Too much to be done. Time enough to play tomorrow. Bubba, go tell your daddy don't wring that bird's neck or else it'll be full of grit."

He cut between the clothes flapping on the line, grimacing when a wet sheet hit his face. His mama'd been bound and determined to get the bedclothes washed, for she wouldn't touch them again until after Old Christmas. Bad luck to wash linen between Christmases, everybody said. Working herself to a frazzle, she was.

He grinned. But come tonight, she'd get a secret smile on her face and light the lamp, adjusting the flame just so before putting the chimney back on, and set it in the window. He'd asked her once when he was little if Baby Jesus was coming to visit, and she'd said serious-like, "The Bible says we don't know the day nor the hour, but we ought to be ready for him to come back, and I always kind of thought it would be fittin' somehow for him to come on his birthday." Then her eyes had crinkled. "After all, that's when he came before!"

A loud squawking shattered his thoughts as Jed came out of the henhouse, carrying a fat chicken by its feet, an ax in his other hand. Bubba backed up a step. He still didn't like seeing one with its head cut off running around the yard, the blood spurting bright red drops into the dust.

"Hey, Bubba," Jed said.

His feet were itching to go. "Mama said to tell you to be sure not to wring that hen's neck." Jed nodded and walked over to the tree stump that served as a chopping block. Bubba hurried away, but not in time to miss hearing the solid *thunk* of the ax.

Dadblame it! He'd stepped right into a pile of chaineyballs, almost slipped and fell. "Scooter!"

"What is it?" Scooter looked around. A gray film covered his face except for the white spot around his nose where he'd wiped it.

"Don't do no good to sweep if you leave them chaineyballs in a pile for somebody to slip on," Bubba snapped, wiping his foot on the doorstep.

Scooter grinned, then, "Bubba? You reckon Israel and Lily be here tomorrow?"

He hedged. "Why don't we just wait and see?"

"Always got to wait and see bout ever'thing," Scooter grumbled as he turned back to his work.

Most likely they wouldn't see hide nor hair of them, Bubba thought, and he didn't know how his parents were gone explain that to Scooter. The Wades had always been there at Christmas. Might as well tell him there wont no Santy Claus.

"Hi-yo, Silver!" Astride the broom, Scooter was galloping down the yard like the Lone Ranger.

Enough, Bubba thought. "Boy, you better finish that sweepin'."

"Okay, Tonto," Scooter called, twirling the broom to a halt. Dismounting, he set to work again, sweeping with a will. Bubba shook his head. Growing up fast — be too old for play and Christmas 'fore we know it. The thought of Scooter's disappointed face and Christmas without Israel and Lily roused an urgency in him that sent him to the house.

He found his mama in the kitchen surrounded by jars of pickles, string beans, and pears. "Mama, you reckon I could slip away for a while?"

Her eyebrows went up. "With all we got to be done? What you got so important it won't wait?"

"Thought I'd go over to Israel's."

"Bubba, you know what your daddy said."

"Yes ma'am. But they might not come over tomorrow, and I done got presents for them, and how else I gone get 'em there?"

She sighed. "I suppose seein' you will be a Christmas present for Lily, all by itself. But don't you be gone long."

Relief washed over him. "I'll take my gun, too. You can tell him I gone huntin'."

120

"If your daddy asks, you know I ain't gone lie," she said. He turned to go. "You'll miss goin' to get the tree."

"I'll be back in time to help set it up."

"See you are. And you might as well carry this." She pulled a small package from the pocket of her sweater hanging by the door. "Just a little something I made for Lily. Tell her I said Happy Christmas."

As Bubba took it, his throat closed and he couldn't speak. Nodding, he went for his gun and coat.

Queen's excitement at the sight of the gun set her nose snuffling among the leaves. "Not yet, girl," Bubba laughed. "Israel's first." The dog barked and dashed ahead. Bubba flapped his coat open in the warm, still air and jammed his red cap in his pocket. Shifting the Browning to cradle the stock more comfortably in his arm, he tramped on.

When he got there, Queen was already barking hello at Lily as she crossed the yard, her empty wash basket balanced on her hip. "Hush that fuss, Queen," she said, "I'se right here." She patted the dog, then nodded, "Hey, Bubba."

Suddenly struck shy, he asked, "Israel around?"

"He gone off to be by hisself awhile, he said. You can cotch him if you're a mind to." She gestured toward the woods. Some strands of her hair had pulled out of her tight braids, and she wiped them back. "Warm, ain't it? Hot Christmas, fat graveyard." Her eye sharpened. "Whatfor you got that big coat on for?"

"Easier to wear than carry."

"Boy ain't got no sense," she muttered. "Take it off. Get overheated this weather, get sick for sure."

Shrugging the coat off, he pulled out the presents. "Here, I brought you all somethin'."

"Lordamercy, what you got there?"

"Just a little Merry Christmas from Mama and me."

"Well, ain't that nice." She turned the basket over and sat on it. Her long fingers fondled the packages. "What's in this one, you reckon?"

"It's from me, and I ain't gone tell."

"Bubba, you is mean." She smiled like the old Lily he'd known. "Can't open it now?"

"Might as well," he laughed. "Know you'll be into it soon's I'm gone anyway."

Her fingers gentle, she pulled away the paper and breathed a soft "Oh" as she lifted the red-purple beads into the air. "Just lookathere. Ain't they purty?"

"Made 'em myself," Bubba mumbled.

"You did?" Lily's eyes were wide. "These are fine, *fine*." She put them on and they caught the sunlight with a red fire. Her hand lifted, hesitated. He smiled. She laid her hand along his cheek. Her lashes were damp. "I thanks you, Bubba. They special 'cause they come from you, from your hand." Bubba beamed, pleased with himself and his present. "Now, you wait just a minute. I got somethin' for you all, too."

"Bring it when you all come tomorrow," he blurted.

She stopped. "Don't know as we will."

"Sure you will. Wouldn't be Christmas without you and Israel, you know that." He babbled fast now. "Look, I got to go, or I won't catch him." He picked up his gun and walked away backward, ignoring the protest starting in her eyes. "Don't you forget now, get there early! Come on, Queen." As the dog rushed to join him, he hollered, "Merry Christmas!" She stood by the upturned basket, holding the beads against her chest like a talisman. He said it again: "Merry Merry Christmas, Lily!" Queen echoed with a yelp and ran into the woods, Bubba on her heels.

14

He marched through the leaves, more determined than ever not to let their Christmas be ruined. A cooling wind set the leaves whirling, and he pulled his coat back on. Queen's bark shrilled as she hit the scent, and a squirrel flattened itself against a maple. Bubba raised the gun and fired, and it fell in a shower of twigs. Queen pranced as he shoved the limp body into his pocket. He patted her neck, "Good girl."

Gray clouds blocked the sun, and a sharp wind made him pull up the collar of his coat. He tramped deeper into the shadowy woods, following Israel's trail, one eye on Queen. Shifting the gun, he found it was wet and looked up, surprised. The light rain misting down had slipped up on him, and the temperature was dropping fast. A chill ran down his back and he shivered.

Suddenly he came upon a clearing of high brush. If he went on into that mess, he'd come out full of stick-tights and sandspurs. The open sky above him was darkening, and he knew he needed to get home. Yet Israel had gone this way, the broken weeds and branches said that. He shrugged and headed in, signaling for Queen to stay put. Quivering in protest, she sat, barely touching the ground. He hardened his heart against her soft whine and elbowed back the dried brush. He heard a voice ahead and moved faster through the drizzle's haze. Then he stopped short at the edge. The clearing dipped into a shallow ravine, and a circle of hard-packed earth lay in front of him with the blackened remains of a fire, stones scattered around it. A broken barrel, Mason jars, pipes, and a rusted black oil drum with its sides caved in littered the ground. An empty cart sat under a gray net of bare vines.

The still. The damned old still that had sent his daddy to jail. He felt like a fist had hit his stomach.

He'd come out on their property, the part Israel said was snake country. Over to the side stood a stack of wood, ready to light a fire that had been doused by the revenuers six years before. The soft burbling of a

124

stream accented the murmurs coming from the man seated on a tree stump. It was Israel, his feet planted square on the ground, shaking his head as he talked to himself. The words came across the cold damp air. "Lord, ain't no man ever been such a fool. No man. No man." He rocked back and forth, working a coiled piece of copper tubing through his hands, and then fell silent.

What fool? What man?

Israel repeated, "Sorry old fool. Sorry old fool," as he bent the tubing into a twist and flung it. The metal clanged as it hit a rock. The tears glinting on his cheeks scared Bubba. He'd never seen Israel cry nor lose his temper.

Then the big man took a large piece of firewood and swung about him, glass flying and metal ringing with each blow. He stopped, his breath vaporing the air, and grabbed the rusty oil drum. With a final cry, he hefted it high, cords swelling in his neck. The drum arced through the air and fell against the cart, shivering the vines, then splashed into the stream.

Head down, hands loose at his sides, Israel stood there amid the broken glass like a man beaten. Time stretched out as the shadows fell. Finally he wiped the back of his hand hard across his cheekbones and left, passing close enough to touch. Bubba ducked down, feeling like he'd just seen his friend naked, and the wrongness of it made him keep quiet and lie low.

He stiffened. What if Israel should see Queen waiting? But no sound came, and then Queen was there, her coat prickly from the brush. The hang of her tail told him she knew something was wrong. He stroked her and picked off some of the sandspurs. Seemed to help somehow, knowing she was as puzzled as he.

When he was sure that Israel was well away, he walked up to the still. The bent copper tubing coiled where it had landed, water drops catching the last light with a red-orange glint, and something in the way the light fell teased his memory. He'd seen it before. In a wagon somewhere, the tow sack that covered it pulled back just enough to see.

The memory came back in a rush. He'd been nosing around like little kids do. He remembered pulling himself up and scraping his shin on the wagon's backboard, and how his foot hit something that made a ringing sound. Squatting, he'd pulled the sack away, and there was the prettiest, thinnest red-gold pipe he'd ever seen. He'd stroked the cold metal's smoothness, but knew he couldn't take it home to play with.

Bubba knelt, his heart drumming as he ran his hand along the cool curve of the pipe. He took a deep breath and let the memory lead him where it would.

Because he already knew. He'd known, deep inside, from the minute he'd seen that pipe in Israel's hands. He'd even recalled its sharp new-metal smell. That pipe had been in Israel's wagon, covered up like a

126

secret. He'd felt uneasy holding a grownup's secret, so he'd scrambled out of the wagon before he got caught and never told anybody what he'd seen, because he'd never connected it with the still. Until now.

A dark sadness, a knowing, welled up inside.

Israel.

He stumbled back through the brush, a startled Queen bounding after him. Stiff wet fronds slapped against his face, cold against his hot skin. He ran on, heedless of potholes, roots, puddles. Once he slipped on the wet leaves, and his thoughts almost caught up with him, but he righted himself, took a firmer grip on his gun, and lit out again. Panic rose in his throat when he realized he couldn't find his way. The woods were full dark now, the rain and sleet coming down harder, soaking into his coat. He jammed on his hat and pulled the earflaps down. Queen leaned against his leg. He knelt, curling his arms around her neck, and let the tears come. He knew he was lost and alone in the woods, and on a black night.

He kept walking, the soaked coat dragging at his shoulders, water squishing inside his boots. The squirrel in his pocket and the Browning were nothing but burdens now, but a gun was too valuable to lose and he needed it to let his daddy know where he was. He'd fired it twice already and yelled for help till his throat felt raw. Then Queen had gone off, and he'd felt uneasy until she came back. After that, he didn't worry if she wandered. He knew she wouldn't leave him. For sure her nose might be a bigger help than his eyes in the dark night.

Finally he sank down at the base of an oak tree, shivering. He'd passed that same tree he didn't know how many times. He could see no moon nor stars, and when he heard a rustling like something bulky moving through the woods, he called, "Queen?" but this time no familiar figure came out of the gloom. Swallowing his fear, he tightened his grip on the gun. A branch snapped, and an odor like sour meat hit his nose. From out of time came Israel's voice: "You watch out in them woods, now, boy. Bears might be out there foraging this time of year." He closed his ears to the remembered voice, but fear drove him to grab a low branch and climb fast, working the gun up ahead of him. Cradled in the high limbs, he stared down into the blackness. Scuffling sounds came up to meet him. For sure a black shadow moved against the dark, and there was the faint gleam of an eye. He wrapped his arms around the clammy tree trunk, wishing it was the chaineyball tree and he was home. He started counting his heartbeats to shut out the thought of what might be waiting below.

After a long time waiting while every shadow and sound set his heart to pounding, a soft whine came from the ground. Queen. "It's all right, girl. I'm up here," he whispered. He heard her plop as she lay down, and relaxed. Ain't no old bear gone come sniffin' around while Queen stands guard. Then he remembered seeing a dog with its innards poking out from the long parallel wounds ripped in its stomach. And Israel's sad voice, "Bear done that, boy. Vicious mean claws they got." But wait — he recalled hearing the men at the store saying no bear had been seen around here in a long time. He swallowed away the bile in his throat. Israel had lied, just like he had about it being snake country.

"Ain't no bears round here now," Bubba said aloud. "That was a long time ago. Israel don't know what he's talkin' bout." The sound of his own voice was reassuring. "Queen's smart. She smell a bear comin', she got sense enough to warn me and get herself out of the way." He was just glad nobody had seen him actin' like a scaredy-cat.

From the road, a car's rumble echoed through the woods, but he couldn't tell which direction it came from. He fired the gun, but the motor faded away. He was cold to his bones, and he had to pee again. Musta peed forty times already. He struggled with the buttons, then stretched out on the limb, the hot drops burning as they came out. He buttoned up quickly and pulled the coat closer. For the first time he could remember, he wasn't praying for snow on Christmas Eve. The thought filled his head with pictures — the warm cinnamon smell of the kitchen, the soft feather bed tucked around his ears, and Scooter's warm back. Then his mind jumped to hot mulled cider and warm sweet potato pie and sillybub that made your innards warm and sent a flush all over. His stomach rumbled.

They prob'ly got the tree all set up by now, and his daddy would come lookin' for him, prob'ly in a temper at having his first Christmas Eve home ruined by some care-for-nothin' boy.

He thought he heard the report of a gun, but then trailing sparks drifted down the black sky. Another burst of fireworks crackled on the cold air, showering a fan of light. Then distant explosions popped all around him — guns, firecrackers, more firecrackers — and gold and red and blue filled the night. Must be near onto midnight, boys setting off their rockets. He recalled Scooter the year before, running around in his long johns, dizzy with excitement to set off the one sparkler that Israel had given him.

The silence was louder than before. He ached with loneliness, and another chill set him shaking. A single ghostly call of a shivering owl broke the quiet. Suddenly he remembered when he was a little boy his daddy going out with his gun — this very one — saying he heard somethin' and was gone shoot who-ever it was stealin' his mule. When the gun went off, Bubba'd waited, his heart in his throat for fear Santy Claus had been shot, and then his daddy came back in, talking gruff, "Well, I missed 'im," and the sweet rush of relief . . . then his parents laughing and his daddy slinging him across his shoulder, saying, "Ain't this how Santy Claus carries his goodies?" and heading up the stairs to tuck him in bed to wait till dawn when he could finally shout "Merry Christmas, Merry Christmas" and pounce on their bed to shake them awake.

Bubba wiped his nose with the back of his hand. Must be Christmas now. Surely his daddy must be looking for him, maybe even with Israel, 'cause he'd need the truck. He tried to ignore the sinking in his stomach. What if Israel suspected he'd found out his secret? He could be lost and never found. He was ashamed to think such, but he couldn't shut out what he'd seen at the still. Then his head came up — he had two good legs and a good dog. They could find their own way out come daybreak, but they needed to seek cover till then. Queen would let him know in plenty of time if anything was coming. He dropped to the ground in a flurry of raindrops. Queen rumbled and nosed his hand. He was so cold, her nose felt warm. "Come on, girl, we got work to do if we gone make it through this night."

He found a sheltered spot and kicked aside the wet top leaves. He took off his coat, the cold shocking his body, and lay down, pulling the coat back over, but no comfort came from its cold weight. Whistling for Queen, he raised the sodden coat, and she plopped down beside him with a sigh. He spread the coat over them and curled up to her long wet back, her soft chest fur warm against his hand. Soon a small glow of body heat came from her, and he scrunched down even closer. Around him the splat of raindrops reminded him how cold he was, and alone. But Queen being there made all the difference, and the smell of wet dog didn't matter. His eyes felt gritty, his body ached, and he dozed.

The light came slowly. Bubba watched the leaves around him take on form. What with dreams about Israel and Ole Raggey and the muskrat's eyes with their yellow gleaming, he'd been afraid to sleep much. The woods were thick with fog, but he could make out skeletal tree shapes now. He watched the drizzle bead and slide down the pine needles, each drop holding more light. Time to get up and make their way out.

Queen raised her head as he shrugged on the cumbersome coat. "Come on, girl. Let's go home." She heaved to her feet with a grunt and almost fell. Bubba rubbed her head. "Good ole girl. You and me gone get through this one, and Israel'll have himself another story to tell." His mind backed away from the words like he'd put a salt finger on a raw wound. Queen whimpered softly, and he noticed her eyes were dull.

A gun went off close by, and he jumped, the stiff body of the squirrel in his pocket hitting his leg. They were looking for him! He raised his gun and fired an answering shot, then tried to run toward the sound, but he couldn't, the sides of his boots were cutting into his legs and his toes were cramping. He clenched his teeth, took one step, then another. Queen moved just

132

as slowly, her gait stiff and her tail down. When he saw the movement in the bushes ahead and caught the wink of a light, he shouted, "Over here!"

The light swung back and forth as a figure came crashing through the underbrush, calling, "Bubba?" and his knees went weak. It was his daddy, wearing a black slicker and an old blue stocking cap on his head. At Queen's soft yelp of welcome, Jed set the kerosene lantern down. "Thank God, thank God," he said, and then Bubba was wrapped in stiff folds of wet rubber and hot tears. Next thing he knew, he was in the air, being carried like a baby, and he didn't mind at all.

15

Israel was waiting at the truck. As Jed lifted Bubba into the front seat, he picked up Queen and put her in the back. "Poor ole dog," he crooned as he threw an old quilt over her. "Poor ole dog."

Bubba was glad to lean away from Israel when his father pulled him closer. Israel slammed the truck into gear and drove them home like the Devil himself was after them. He only spoke once on the jolting ride, asking, "You all right, boy?" and Bubba nodded against the wet slicker and shut his burning eyes. Be a fine time to tune up like some baby, now it was all over.

Next thing he knew they were in Lily's kitchen in front of the fire, the men cutting the boots from his legs. He saw the steam rising from his clothes, clouds of it, as he drank the cup of hot soup Lily put in his hands, and then his mama pulled his hat off, making soft sounds of distress. And here came Lily again with her good quilt, saying, "Get them clothes off, boy, and wrop yourself up."

"Hold your horses, Lily," Israel said. "First we gotta get these boots off'n his feet. He swole all up."

Ruby clucked her tongue as she started toweling Bubba's hair dry. "Ow!" He tried to pull away.

"Just you hold on, young man. I don't want to hear no word from you — what we been through this night!" Ruby said, and attacked his hair again.

"Ain't no point rubbin' him bald, Ruby," Jed said.

"Got to do something, him so soaked, and will you look?" She held out the red-streaked towel for them to see. Israel looked up at Bubba and started to laugh. At Bubba's scowl, Lily gently turned his head. "Looka-there, boy. What you see?" In the spotted dresser mirror, he saw a red band across his forehead and more red streaks down his cheeks. Stains from that ole hat. He touched his head, and his fingers came away red, too. Don't look so funny to me. Reckon it's on there permanent?

When all his clothes were off, Lily wrapped him in the warm quilt. His mama dragged over a pan of hot water, and once his feet were in it, the pins-and-needles feeling eased. His feet looked white and bloated, and a neat crisscross pattern of grooves marched up his shins where the bootlaces had tied. As he sipped at the hot soup, the warmth came at him from both ends, and the shivering finally stopped. Queen lay stretched out in front of the fire, her coat in prickles from the quick toweling Israel had given her. His eyes filled, and he blinked. Ole dog didn't know how special she was, for Lily to let her lay on her good rug.

He looked down at Israel's curly head as the man massaged his leg. The play of muscles across his shoulders suddenly brought back the vision of his arms lifting the steel drum. His daddy was working on his other leg. The two heads were side by side, and brown hands worked next to white hands just like they had in that story Lily told about Israel pullin' his daddy out of that old well. He could tell from the warm feeling in the room that peace had been made between the two men, and the tension of the last weeks was gone. But it had come too late for him, for he couldn't go back to the way it used to be. He felt like a stranger, watching them and knowing what he knew. The sadness pressed on his shoulders like a burden, and a weariness washed over him.

Then Scooter stood in the doorway, his cowlick

standing up, his eyes puffy with sleep. He rubbed his face. "Has Bubba got found yet?"

Bubba sat up, untangling himself from the quilt cocoon. "I'm right here."

Scooter's mouth opened. Putting his head down, he charged straight for his brother. He butted into the quilt with an "oomph" and wrapped his arms around Bubba. When he didn't look up right away, Bubba pulled at his hair to raise his head. The boy's face was tear-streaked, his eyes accusing. "Where you been? You were gone and we had got the tree and Mama had popped corn all ready to string and it started rainin' and you and Queen didn't come back . . ." he stopped for breath, "and where you *been?*"

"Up a tree."

The boy swiped an angry fist at his eyes. "This ain't no time for pickin' on me, Bubba."

Lord, he sounds so growny, Bubba thought. "I ain't pickin'."

"A tree? In the woods?"

"For sure." Bubba realized everyone was listening, and his ears got hot. Daggone it, what'd I go and tell that for? If he knew Scooter, the next thing out of his mouth was gone be why.

"Why?" Scooter said.

He mumbled, "Thought I heard a bear."

"A bear? A real bear?"

"Not a real bear," Bubba said. "Just *thought* I heard

136

a bear. Forgot none been seen this long while." He stared at Israel, challenging him to say different.

But the man just nodded, "That's a fact."

"But you missed Christmas Eve!" Then, realizing what he'd said, he shouted, "Hey, everybody, it's Christmas!" He jumped up, "Come on, Bubba, let's go home. Wonder what Santy Claus brought?"

"Hold on, boy," Jed said. "First we got to go get your brother some dry clothes."

Ruby stroked Bubba's hair. "I got *my* Christmas present, my boy home safe and sound."

Following Jed out, Israel came back to put a hand on Bubba's shoulder. "Glad you made it back here, boy. Night lost in the woods in winter ain't no pleasure for man nor beast." When Bubba didn't answer, Israel shook his shoulder. "You hear me?"

"Yeah," he said, but he kept his eyes on his swollen feet. He didn't want to look in Israel's eyes again for fear the man would see what he knew, and he didn't want Israel to know that. Not yet.

In all the excitement of opening Christmas presents and eating, nobody questioned why Bubba stayed so quiet. The Wades had been with them all day, and he wished they'd go home so he could think. But his mama sat firm in her rocker with the family Bible on her lap, the lamp aglow behind her. She licked her thumb to turn the thin pages and with a smile started reading the Christmas story. Her soft voice lulled Bubba. From when he was little, she'd read in such a way it made it all real, and he would almost believe he could go out and find people in the barn, and one of them a baby.

He looked around the room. The cedar Christmas tree had arcs of colored paper chains and popcorn strings, and every blank spot was loaded with soap-suds snow. His eyes flicked past Israel to Lily, who was nodding as if she were pleased the Bible story hadn't changed. He realized his father was staring at him, but then Jed nodded as if satisfied and turned his attention back to Ruby. Even Scooter, still holding the small wagon his daddy had made, listened as he sat cross-legged under the tree. It was all the same, yet not the same. Bubba still felt a chill inside where the fire couldn't touch.

His mama had reached the part about Herod and the three kings, and how ole Herod told them to let him know where they found the Baby Jesus so he could go worship him too, and all the while him knowing he was telling a lie, 'cause he had murder in his heart for that child. Tell one thing and do another.

Bubba remembered how Israel had always had an avoiding look whenever he'd asked why his daddy had to go to jail, and how he'd stayed away from them at first. And the night before his daddy came home, how Israel had worked that hat around and around. That wont like him, but now Bubba knew why: Israel had known he'd done wrong, lettin' his friend take the blame and him guilty as sin. All the while he was helpin' them out and teachin' Bubba things and takin' his love, it had been an act like ole Herod's, just guilt making him do those things. Tell one thing and do another.

Bubba felt his stomach roll, and not from the gritty chill tonic his mama had made him take. The sense of betrayal and loss cut so sharp he studied the blue knit scarf in his lap so no one could see his face. Lily now. Lily had made him this scarf, and he didn't doubt every stitch had been made with her true love. And her married to someone like Israel. Well, like as not she didn't know.

His mama closed the Bible, rubbing her hand across the worn leather. Everyone sat quiet as the clock whirred and chimed eight strokes. Israel looked at him, but Bubba glanced away as if he didn't see. The big man got to his feet and smoothed his pants legs down. "This has sure been a Christmas to remember," he said, "but we best be gettin' on home. I'll just take a look at Miss Queen on my way out."

Jed nodded. "I put her in the barn. Thought it'd be a mite warmer there."

"I can take care of her," Bubba said, sharper than he meant. He didn't want Israel touching her.

His father looked at him, surprised. "Well, I reckon

you can, but you know good as me that Israel got a way
with dogs. Best medicine Queen could have, feelin'
Israel's healin' hands on her."

Scooter looked up from his wagon. "She ain't gone
die, is she, Israel?"

"Now don't you start in worryin' about that, Squirt.
Miss Queen, she been through worse than this. 'Spect
she'll be just fine, onct she gets warm."

Bubba felt his worry ease. But he was still gone
check on her first thing in the morning. With the
Wades calling a last "Happy Christmas," Ruby and
Jed walked them out. Bubba sighed in relief and
looked over at Scooter. The boy was curled up asleep
beside the tree, the wagon still in his hand.

His parents came back in on a gust of cold air.
"Looks like this one's engine finally run down," Jed
said with a wide grin as he scooped the boy up in his
arms. Ruby lit the way upstairs, and Jed followed, his
hand sheltering Scooter's head.

Bubba stretched. He ought to go to bed, too, but he
hated to move. All he'd wanted all day was to be alone,
and now the time had come, he was reluctant to leave
the room with its evergreen smell. He wished he'd
been the one to give Scooter the pair of shoes that
rested side by side on the dime-store cotton. Brand
spankin' new they were, and that meant the rest of the
prison money was prob'ly gone. He heard the truck rev
up outside. Queen must be all right. His mama came

downstairs. "Best you go on up, too, Bubba. You near bout asleep where you sit."

"Yes'm," he said, and got stiffly to his feet. He limped to give her a kiss. "Happy Christmas, Mama."

"Sweet dreams, son. Remember your prayers."

Upstairs in the pool of yellow lamplight, Jed was tucking the quilt around Scooter. Bubba slid in the bed, shivering as the cold feather bed closed around him. "You too big to be tucked in?" his daddy asked. He tucked the quilt under the mattress, and Bubba sighed. Maybe this one night Scoot couldn't pull the covers off. "Bubba?" Jed sat on the edge of the bed. "You want to talk about what happened last night?"

"Ain't much to tell."

"You been mighty quiet."

It blurted out. "I found the still."

Jed's head pulled back, but then he nodded. "Surprised you haven't run up on it before now."

"Ain't all . . ." he bit his lip. The scene came back so sharp he suddenly didn't want to talk about it.

"Ain't all what?"

What if Israel had put his daddy up to building that still? Lily always said where you see one, you see the other. "Nothin'. Whatfor anybody want to build a still anyhow? Didn't they know they might get caught?"

Jed hesitated. "Maybe they felt it was worth takin' that chance for some money. You too young to remember, son, but it was hard times back then. A man's

141

family's hungry or about to lose their land for taxes, the difference between right and wrong gets mighty thin." Bubba knew about taxes. But best he could remember, they hadn't been behind on taxes when the still was found, and they hadn't been hungry neither. Nor had Israel. He realized his father was studying his face. Jed sighed. "Son, I didn't have nothin' to do with that still. I thought you knew that. It's just that I can see how a man could get that desperate."

Then that meant Israel had built it all by himself, and that meant he wont the man Bubba'd thought he was. Like his daddy was different from what he remembered. His confused thoughts settled down into a loneliness stronger than any he'd ever known. He forced the rising ache back. "Why'd they have to build it on our land?"

"Got to have a good hidey-hole with water. That's what matters, not whose land it's on."

"It wont right you had to go to jail instead of them." He waited, then asked with his heart beating a slow thud. "Do you know who it was?"

"No. Makes no nevermind now."

But Bubba knew, and he minded a lot. "You and Israel gone be friends again?"

Jed shot him a sharp look. "Israel and me ain't never stopped bein' friends."

"But you didn't want us to see him no more."

Jed nodded. "I had my reasons. I'd got to thinkin' we were too beholden, but last night proved me wrong.

You might still be lost in those woods but for him. Taught me beholden ain't got nothin' to do with friendship." Bubba kept silent, and he went on, "Then, too, it seemed like you all got a tough enough row to hoe because I went to jail, without bein' looked down on because we're friends with colored."

"That don't matter," Bubba said.

"Not to us, but it does to some folks."

Scooter mumbled in his sleep and turned over. When he quieted down again, Jed continued, his voice softer. "It was one thing for your mama to be takin' help from the Wades when I wont here. Some think colored ain't here for nothin' but to help out white. But now I'm home, they figure we ought not need their help." He looked off, like he could see the Wades' house through the bedroom wall. "I was tryin' to do what was best for us and them, too."

"Just because what some folks might say?"

Jed's eyes were steady. "Or do. People don't like it when somebody upsets their ways of thinkin'. They get scared, and scared folks can get mean."

"You talkin' bout the Klan?"

"Partly. The Klan ain't the only ones end up hatin' and hurtin'."

"You think somebody would hurt Israel and Lily?"

"Wouldn't be the first time talk led to trouble and regrets come after."

"Like when Benjamin died?"

"You remember that?" Bubba nodded. "Guess you

do. It was just before they found the still, and you remember all that, don't you?"

He stared down at the quilt. "Yes sir."

"A long time ago, that night. For sure they never meant to kill a child, but you start hatin' and things gone happen, meant or no. Broke Israel's and Lily's hearts. They set some store by that boy."

Him, too. Benjamin had been his best friend. "What'd the Klan have against Israel anyway?"

"Just that he was colored and owned his own land."

Bubba blinked. If those men knew what he knew, they'd be after Israel for sure. They wouldn't have no truck with a colored man sending a white to jail. If his daddy had known, he wouldn't have had to go at all.

Jed patted him on the hip. "Colored or not, friends is friends, and the Wades and the Harkinses have gone through a lot together. They've proved themselves more than true." Bubba bit down hard on his tongue, for he knew if he opened his mouth he'd tell. As Jed picked up the lamp, Bubba looked away from the light. "Glad you're back home safe, son. Good night."

He got out a muffled "Night" and watched the lamp's glow as it faded down the stairs. His body ached, and the secret burned like a hot coal in his chest. He stared into the black with gritty eyes, then pushed his head into the pillow and cried.

16

Rain. It hadn't done anything but rain for three days, and Bubba was sick of it. Queen didn't seem to be getting any better, and every day when Israel had been over to check her, Bubba had avoided him, but he sometimes felt the man watching him with puzzled eyes.

He stepped up onto the porch with his bucket of eggs, and a cold drop snaked its way down his neck. The yard ran with yellow rivulets, and his boots were already heavy with clay. A gust shook the gleaming black branches of the chinaberry tree, showering fat drops into the steady drizzle. The few berries left shone gold against the lowering clouds.

In the distance, he heard someone singing, a sad, lonely sound that fitted the day. Out of the mist, a mule-drawn wagon took shape on the road, loaded high with a chifforobe and bedstead and pans tied to the side. A man and woman, backs bent against the rain, rode on the bench, and lined up on the wagon's rear, four children held a quilt above their heads for shelter. The woman sang slow and soft, "Swing low, sweet chariot . . ." as the man hummed along. She ignored the giggling children behind her as they tugged at the cover. The wagon's wheels dipped into a rut, setting the furniture tilting and the pans clanging.

"Tenants." Ruby had come to the kitchen door. "Bad day for movin'." Bubba scraped his feet and stepped into the warmth. At the table, Scooter was practicing his writing, his pencil gripped tight. "First one I've seen this week," Ruby said, closing the door. " 'Spect there'll be more soon enough. Thank the Lord it ain't bad as it used to be."

"Folks got to be crazy, move in weather like this," Scooter said with an exaggerated shiver.

"Some people ain't got no choice, son," Ruby said. "We're blessed — we own our land. But them folks don't, and come the end of the year, if the landlord says go, then they got to find some other place."

"That ain't fair," Scooter said.

"Raggey says it's fair," Bubba muttered. "You work for hire, you don't work, you don't get hired."

"Now Bubba," Ruby said, her eyebrows drawn tight, "you know it ain't always like that. Why, I seen the day didn't matter how hard you worked, farms would fail. Banks were foreclosin', and these roads would be full 'tween Christmas and New Year's, just one wagon after another, alookin' a new place and better days."

And Ole Raggey most likely buyin' up their land, Bubba thought, remembering the talk at the store.

"We ain't gone lose our place, are we, Mama?" Scooter asked. "This here's home."

"Not if your daddy has anything to say about it." When Bubba shivered like a ghost had walked on his grave, she said, "Son, you need to get yourself dry."

"In a minute. I want to go check on Queen first."

"Carry her this, then." She handed him a dish. "Made her up some mush. See if she'll take it." The bowl warmed Bubba's hand. His mama set some store by Queen. "She any better this mornin'?"

He shook his head. "About the same."

"Wish this rain would stop," she said. "Damp ain't good for sickness, man nor beast."

As Bubba went out, Scooter said, "She'll be all right, Mama. Israel said ole dogs just take longer."

Israel better be right, Bubba thought as he crossed the yard. He hadn't been to see her yet today, and Bubba caught himself wishing he would hurry; he didn't like the way Queen had looked this morning. Her eyes were rheumy, and when she relieved herself, she squatted like every muscle ached, and came right back to the old quilt spread on the corn shucks they'd scooped up for a bed. She wasn't hearing right, either. When he'd touched her, she'd jumped, startled, and then licked his hand.

But still she had seemed some better than yesterday. She'd been racked then with chills so bad Israel had dosed her again and rubbed her down, talking to

147

her soft, "All right, girl. I knows you hurtin', and Israel's gone fix that." Bubba had tensed up at him touching her, but held himself back because Israel did have a way of soothing an animal. Queen had a trusting look on her face as he worked his hands over her that Bubba couldn't understand. He'd always heard dogs could tell about people better than people could. Finally the shaking had stopped and she eased into sleep. Healing sleep, Israel had called it.

But today when he'd slipped a bit of chicken meat into her mouth, she just let it lay there until he picked it up, her eyes looking for all the world like saying she was sorry. Her who had always been so partial to chicken.

Wont fair, he thought. He didn't even get a cold from their lost night, and she be so sick.

The rain-soaked barn door creaked as he pulled it partway open and slipped in. In the silence, the drizzle tapped softly on the tin roof, and the cold damp struck through his sweater. Queen hadn't even tried to worm her way out from under the quilt, much as she hated being covered. He remembered the time Scooter dressed her up and how they'd laughed till his mama took pity. Once free, Queen had run off like she'd had pepper on her tail.

He grinned at the memory as he leaned over to place the mush near her head, but then something in her stillness froze his smile. "Queen?" He reached to touch her and saw her eyes were open, but like she wasn't there. His own eyes stung and blurred as he put his hand gently to her chest and felt again and again for a heartbeat, ignoring the cold feel of her body against his palm. No throb came.

He sat on the floor and eased her body up into his lap. The pine-sap smell of Israel's liniment came strong, but there was still a Queen smell. He smoothed the black hair, noticing the short, stiff strands of white around her mouth. Softly he stroked her while his hot tears fell. As the rain pattered on the roof, he rocked her back and forth, pulling the quilt up around her, whispering "Queen," then "Queen" again, and then there was silence.

When he saw the light, he knew they had come to find him. He hoped it was his mama. His tears finally dry, he'd sat there as darkness fell, still cradling Queen's heavy body, not yet willing to let her go.

The light came closer, and his father stood in the doorway, holding the black slicker over his head. "Bubba, you in there?" He came in closer. The bright pool of light made Bubba blink and look away.

"Bubba?"

"Queen," was all he could get out.

Jed put the lantern down and squatted beside him. He touched Queen's head, his hand shaking. "Let me have her," he said, and there was such a note in his voice that Bubba handed over the burden into his arms, quilt and all. His tears welled again when he saw the love in his daddy's face as he gently ran his finger along the bridge of Queen's nose. When he bowed his head and turned his face away, Bubba leaned into him, and Jed's free arm came around the boy's shoulders. Then Bubba felt his father's head rest on his own, and a shudder ran down Jed's body. "She was a good dog," he said. Bubba nodded against his arm. In the circle of light, he saw his father's hand stroking, stroking the quilt.

A truck rumbled into the yard, its headlights tracing a yellow arc across the open barn door. The engine choked to a stop, then the metal door slammed, but Jed didn't move, just let his breath out slow. "Israel's here," he said. Bubba pulled back, swiping at his face. He didn't want to see Israel, but he wouldn't leave Queen.

"Mist Jed? You in there?" He must have seen them, he kept on coming. "Saw the light and figured this where you might be. How Miss Queen doin'?"

Bubba saw Israel's muddied boots as they came closer, then stopped.

"Oh Lordy, oh Lordy, ain't gone tell me Miss Queen gone?" He bent over and touched the dog in Jed's arms. "Poor ole dog. Just couldn't make it this time."

Bubba looked at the brown hand on the black fur

and at Israel shaking his head, the raindrops like specks of light falling off the brim of his hat.

"She's dead," Bubba said.

Israel nodded and pulled off the hat. "And I'm sorry as I can be, Bubba."

"You said she wouldn't die."

"Son, you know he did all he could," Jed said.

His bitterness spilled out. "Wont good enough, was it?" The rain had even made Israel's eyes look wet, but he couldn't fool Bubba. Tell one thing and do another. And now Queen was gone as well.

"Bubba, you know I love that dog good as my own. I wouldn't do nothin' to harm her."

He didn't know what was true anymore and what was not. Only thing he knew for sure was Queen was dead, and Israel had said she wouldn't die. When the big man reached toward him, he jumped up. "Don't you touch me. And don't you touch her, ever again. I don't want to hear no more bout no healin' hands."

Israel's face went slack. Bubba saw the hurt being pushed back and a guard drop over his eyes. "Whatever you say, *Mista* Bubba."

"That's enough!" Jed's voice startled them both. "I don't know what's got into you two, but this ain't the place nor time. This here's Queen we got layin' here, and she deserves our respect. Fightin' over her body ain't no way to repay her for all these years."

Bubba felt ashamed. Here was Queen, his own

Queen, lying limp and gone, and he fussin' with some old colored man what wasn't worth it.

Jed struggled to his feet, still holding the dog's body in his arms. He looked at Israel, the pain bare in his eyes. "You help me bury her?" Israel's face softened, and he nodded. Bubba looked straight ahead.

Scooter wanted to do it right, and so the next morning he and Bubba took Ruby's Bible and went behind the barn to where the raw earth still showed the spade marks. With swollen eyes, Scooter stood shivering in the cold mist, and holding the book tight against his chest, he recited every Bible verse he'd learned by heart at Sunday school. None of them made much sense to Bubba — they didn't have anything to do with Queen dying — but they hadn't made any sense at Benjamin's funeral either, he'd been so little. Yet he took comfort now as he had then in their sound and in his brother's high voice as he repeated the words against the icy wind. After they said the Lord's Prayer, Scooter patted the damp soil and choked out "Goodbye, Queen." As they walked away, the boy slipped his hand into his brother's, and Bubba blinked hard. If Scooter saw tears, he'd tune up all over again, and he'd cried enough the night before.

He'd sat with Bubba while his daddy and Israel dug, his body shaking until Bubba had taken him inside his own coat to share his body heat. He'd had to let him go while he and his daddy lowered Queen, and that's when Scooter's tears had really started to come. Israel had picked him up and held him while Bubba and Jed filled the hole. Bubba hadn't cried; he'd felt dead himself inside until he saw Israel pick up his little brother, and then the bitterness came burning again. He'd wanted to grab Scooter right out of his arms, but Queen had to come first right then.

He'd noticed that Israel had been careful not to touch her, just helped dig the hole, and he'd felt guilty but glad at the same time. Don't want him messin' with me or mine anymore. I got my reasons.

Scooter jerked his hand. "Bubba, didn't you hear what I said?" He looked at the boy blankly. "I said Israel said he's gone help us find another puppy, said he thought Queen would like that." When Bubba didn't answer, he went on, "I ain't never had a little puppy before. Maybe it'll grow up to be just like Queen."

"Ain't no dog gone ever be like Queen."

Scooter paused. "Well, maybe *almost* like Queen."

Bubba didn't feel like arguing. He didn't want another dog. Let Scooter have one if it made him feel better, but no puppy could ever take the place of Queen. And for sure he didn't want nothin' Israel had to offer.

17

I hate February, Bubba thought, head down and shoulders hunched as he strode across the yard. Everything froze up and gray, nothin' to do after school but sit in the house and try to keep warm, or else get out in the cold to do chores. Cold or not, ditch banks had to be shrubbed, the garden burned off, and now his father had stuck him with the mess of cleaning out the chicken house. He'd planned to clean it out anyway, and he didn't like being told.

He and his father had already knocked heads once this morning. Jed had wanted Scooter out helping, but Bubba had told him his mama wanted him to stay inside and do homework. At that, Jed had said, "Work around here comes first. Your mama's been coddlin' him too much." And that was all it took for Bubba to flare in his mama's defense, "Scooter ain't spoiled. He's done his share since he was little. Mama's always said schoolwork comes first." And Jed had snapped back, "That's enough. I don't know what splinter's got into you lately, but you ain't talkin' that way to me." And he'd gone to the house for Scooter.

Still scowling, Bubba grabbed the pitchfork from the

154

side of the barn. A pile of manure flew out the door, landing in the wagon parked nearby. Suddenly, getting the droppings out of the henhouse didn't look so bad. He could be in there shoveling the heavy manure, with his father staying in back of him every minute, finding fault with what he was doing. He saw Israel jab his pitchfork into another pile and toss it, then pull out his handkerchief to wipe his forehead. It was the red one that Bubba had given him for Christmas.

An abrupt pain got Bubba moving, and he hurried to the henhouse. A door slammed, and he saw Scoot hurtling down the path, his legs pumping, the long scarf Ruby had tied around his neck flapping in the wind. Israel came out of the barn and ruffled Scooter's hair. The boy grinned, hopping from one foot to the other, but Bubba could only hear the sound of their voices, not the words.

Israel and me must have looked like that when I was little, he thought, and looked away. A bird called across the still winter air as he watched an eagle soar in a slow circle in the sky above him. He remembered how, on days when they were bone tired, his mama used to read aloud that part in the Bible about how if they waited on the Lord, He'd renew their strength and they'd mount up with wings as eagles and not be weary.

He sighed. But even with his daddy home, seemed like that wont never gone come true. He still felt borne down to the ground. Sometimes he thought he'd explode with the secret, felt like he ought to say

155

something to his father, he set such innocent store by Israel's friendship. He wondered what Israel thought of such a foolish man.

"Bubba," Scooter ran up, excited, "Israel's gone teach me how to fish, come spring!"

"You want to know how to fish, I can teach you."

"But Israel said he would." He looked at his brother, puzzled. "Bubba, don't you like him anymore?"

"Sure, I like Israel fine."

"You ain't been actin' like it."

"Ain't no such." He started into the henhouse.

"You still blamin' him bout Queen?"

Lordamercy, he hadn't said one word to him about Queen. "Where you get a notion like that?"

"You ain't acted the same since she died. And I heard Mama and Daddy talkin'." He should have known, Bubba thought. "Wont Israel's fault she died," Scooter went on. "Daddy says he got healin' hands."

"He ain't God, Scooter. Israel's just a plain old dirt farmer like us, and he don't know everything."

"He knows more'n I know, and more'n you know, and more'n Daddy knows. Daddy told me so."

"But he don't know everything," Bubba snapped, then hushed. Scooter would see Israel's true colors in time. He wont stupid. "Have it your way," Bubba muttered, and marched into the henhouse.

The season turned the corner into March, and one early morning Bubba woke to radiant light coming through the windows and the quilt turned white overnight. When he moved, a dark seam ran down the covers. "Scoot," he whispered, "wake up slow and don't move."

Scooter's eyelashes flickered. Then he sat bolt upright, eyes wide. "Snow!" He bounced on the bed, flapping the covers and sending the snow powder whirling. The fine flakes had drifted in under the shake roof during the night, dusting the room. The boy's feet left dark prints on the floor as he ran to the window. "There's icicles everywhere, Bubba, even hangin' off the trees! And *everything* is white!"

A sun's ray sent patterns of light flickering around the room from the glazed chinaberries on the tree outside. For the first time in weeks, Bubba felt his burden lift. Winter wont so bad when a snow fell. And a March snow meant spring was coming.

Scooter was throwing on his clothes. "We got to hurry 'fore Israel gets here for the snowfight with Daddy."

"He gone stay in the warm if he's got good sense."

"Huh, that's what you think. Sometimes you act like you don't know Israel at all," Scooter said, and he was gone down the stairs yelling, "Snow! Snow evcrybody!"

Bubba sighed and shook his head. Lily's stories. They had made their daddy real for Scooter while he was gone, stories of how him and Israel grew up together and how they'd steal biscuits from Lily's kitchen when they went huntin', and have snowfights, even when they were grown. "They closer than blood kin," Lily used to say. "Ain't nothin' one wouldn't do for the other."

He could remember some from when he was little, but most of his memories were just bits and pieces. It was Lily who painted the pictures so real he even remembered things he didn't recall. Her tales had helped keep his daddy close and alive in his mind. He could picture the two men together, and whenever he had seen Israel, it was like seeing his daddy, too, somehow.

But things had changed, and now the sight of the man only brought back the hurt of that Christmas Eve and the weight of the secret he was carrying. He'd have to tell Scoot not to put too much stock in those old stories. He bet Israel wont gone come for any snowfight this day, anyway. He rolled out of bed and pulled on his overalls quick before the cold could get past his underwear.

But Israel had come. Horn blaring, the truck pulled in, snow piled on top and a cleared peephole on the wind-shield, and Lily waving. Jed's face split in a grin as he went out. "Wondered when you'd get here."

"Figured I'd bring them sleds over for the boys, and Lily and Miss Ruby could visit," Israel said.

"Tell a lie. You ain't never been able to stay away from snow in your whole life," Jed laughed.

Bubba felt Scooter looking at him and knew a smirk

was on his face. He didn't look back. He wasn't going to give him a chance to say "I told you so."

Lily came in smelling of sharp clean air, and Ruby got her some coffee. "Wondered if you all would come. Jed's been half watchin' that road all morning."

"Don't doubt. Israel was rarin' to come right after breakfast. Chores had to be done first, though."

Bubba looked out the window just as a snowball flew through the air from behind the truck. It hit his father square in the chest as he came out the door pulling on his coat. Jed threw his arms up and shouted, "No fair!" Running low, he scooped up a handful of snow, while snowballs soared above him.

"Snowfight! Snowfight!" Scooter cried.

"Some boys don't never grow up," said Lily, shaking her head, but her voice had a smile in it.

Israel had a line of snowballs ready and waiting on the running board, but when he peeked up to throw another one, a mound of snow hit him in the back, and he laughed for sheer joy. "Who's the sorry thing now? Sneakin' around behind my back!" and he let fly in the direction of the chinaberry tree. Jed ducked back. "You man enough to come out from behind that tree?"

"You man enough to come out from behind that truck?"

"I man enough."

"Believin' is seein'."

Jed had been working steady and now had a pile of

159

snowballs that he threw one after the other as Israel ran from the barrage. Bubba couldn't believe his eyes. There were two grown men, one colored, one white, running around in the snow acting like two dern fools. Grownups ought to have more sense, he thought. But maybe being grown-up didn't mean you had any more sense than you had to start with.

"They'll get cold pretty soon and come in wantin' coffee and anything else warm they can get their hands on," Ruby said.

"That's right," Lily said, laughing. "You boys be lucky you don't get a cold hand down your backs."

"They ain't gone touch me." Scooter dived under the table just as boots stomped on the porch. "They're comin'," he cried, curling into a ball.

"Scoot, quit actin' so silly and come out from under there," Bubba said.

Scooter looked up too fast and cracked his head. "I ain't bein' silly."

The two men, dusted with snow, came in laughing on a rush of cold air, rubbing their hands. "Wooo, I needs to get these hands warm. Come here, woman," Israel said, stalking Lily.

"Get away with yourself, Israel Wade. You ain't puttin' no cold hands on me," she backed off, laughing.

"Who else we got warm in this here room then?" His glance shied away from Bubba, then lit on Scooter backing on all fours under the table again. "Well, lookahere. Just what I need, a nice toasty-warm boy."

"No, no," Scooter yelled, squirming as Israel held him and put his hands on his neck, ignoring his fuss.

"My, my, don't that feel good? Reckon I could find me another warm spot?" and amid the giggling squeals, he tickled the boy's sides and finally put him down. Israel had done that to him once, Bubba remembered. Caught him crying for his daddy down by the creek and started acting silly to make him laugh. He'd tickled him till Bubba cried laughing tears, and then swung him up to ride piggyback on his shoulders. He strode across the field singing, Bubba bouncing and feeling like the king of the world, he was up so high. When they got home, Israel set him in the chinaberry tree, and Bubba'd had to climb down. He'd looked up at the big man who seemed to stretch clear into the sky, and Israel had told him, "Remember, always walk tall, boy. You look at the ground all the time, you trips over your own feets." Bubba blinked back the memory. Lily handed Israel some coffee. "You quit your messin' and warm up your ownself, you plan to go out again with these boys."

They'd made a snowman and ridden the sleds the rest of the afternoon. Then Scooter had disappeared until Bubba found him by the barn solemnly making a dog out of snow on Queen's grave, his ears red with cold and his nose runny. He'd finally gotten the boy back to the house, after he'd promised to help him finish the statue the next day.

Now Scooter was asleep in Jed's lap in the kitchen,

161

and the melted remains of snow cream were drying into yellow streaks on the dishes. Bubba smiled as Lily and his mama laughed softly at the sink. At least one good thing had come out of that Christmas night. He let the drone of voices drift over him, half-asleep himself from the warmth. Then he heard Israel say, "You decided what you gone do bout the taxes?" and his eyes opened.

Jed shook his head. "Have to let it ride another year. 'Spect they'll give us some breathin' time?"

" 'Magine so," Israel nodded. "Not like it has been. Times is better now, and they figure folks will pay soon's they can."

"Thought it might be that way. Can't get blood out of a turnip." Jed sipped his coffee. Silence fell, the only sound the clink of dishes and the murmuring of the women's voices. "Things all right to your place?"

"We'll get by. You need somepin', you let me know."

" 'Preciate that. But best we cut our own row."

Bubba was relieved. He didn't want them to take any help from Israel. He let his eyes close again and the voices fade behind his thoughts.

Taxes. Wont one thing, it was another. When his daddy had left, the county had let 'em ride at first, but then his mama said they were talkin' a sheriff's sale, and there wont nothin' for it but to sell ole Lightnin'. They could get by with the one mule they had left. But then Maypop had died, and things went from bad to worse, and his mama wouldn't touch the mule money

162

that was left, she held that for taxes to come till it was used up. If Israel hadn't come helpin' out, he didn't know where they would have ended up. He shut out the memory pictures on his closed eyelids. Best forget those times. That was shame help, not friend help. He bet if his father knew what he knew, he wouldn't have laughed and played with Israel like he'd done that day. He would've thought twice.

But maybe not. He didn't seem to have the pride he used to have. Seemed like it had been whipped out of him by goin' to prison. And all because of a man he'd called friend. A great sadness washed over Bubba. For the first time, he felt sorry for his father.

18

Bubba took a deep breath of the softening air as he ambled along, rolling his shoulders in pleasure at the warming sun. Patches of snow still lay in the shade, but his quick eye picked out the light green blossoms just opening on the dogwoods, and sprigs of sorrel hinting blue against the fiddlehead ferns curving their way out of the earth. He left the road, remembering a patch of dandelions he'd seen, his mouth watering at the thought of fresh greens after the winter of pantry food. Then he spotted Lily's familiar figure stooping in the Wade family graveyard. Every spring she weeded it out first thing. Likely she was thinking on Benjamin and felt heavy-hearted. He changed his course.

She looked up, her poke bonnet dangling down her back by its string. "Hey, Bubba. Don't this sun feel good? Where you headin'?"

"Huntin' some dandelions."

"Woo-oo, some dandelion salat be good." She patted the greening grass. "Sit a spell."

He dropped down beside her. Early violets peeked out from their heart leaves. "You spring cleanin'?"

She glanced at the graves. "I ain't gone have my Benjamin lyin' in no briers." She tilted her head. "You know, every time I looks at you, I wonder what he'd be lookin' like now. He just a year younger, you remember?" He nodded. "You two were bout close as your daddy and Israel." Bubba flinched, but she didn't see. "He sure did look forward to your playtimes."

He smiled, remembering the laughing boy. "Seemed like we stayed in trouble most times."

"Huh," Lily smiled. "Likeliest pair of devils I ever did see. Wont in one mess, startin' another." Her eyes got their remembering look, but not the sad one she usually had. Maybe it did her good to talk like this. He usually didn't know what to say when she mentioned Benjamin. He tried to call up a memory to make her smile.

164

"Bet you don't remember when we dumped water on Israel's head out in the barn."

She gave him a push, laughing. "Lordamercy, you don't reckon I forgets that? That Israel, he come in just a sputterin'. Didn't help none when I started into laughin' neither. And you boys done give yourselfs slam away with all that gigglin' from under the house."

"We figured he couldn't reach us there."

"Huh. First he fuss, then he start into laughin' hisself, and say leave you there, you come out when you gets hungry enough." She smiled, "You all sure did brighten our days." She ran her hands across the soft violets, her smile fading. "My boy, he sure did love flowers. This year I'm gone plant some wildflowers all over this place. You think he'd like that?"

" 'Spect so." Bubba still kept a dried seed cage they'd found among his treasures.

"Hurtin' thing to think of a boy what loved pretty things so good dyin' like he done. Fire wont pretty to him — sight of it enough to set him screamin' since he was a baby on my hip. Almost like he knew . . ."

He'd never been told Benjamin died by fire. His face must have given him away, for Lily's hand flew to her mouth. "Oh Bubba, I forgot. I'm sorry, child." Her tears brimmed. "Seem like lately I gets to thinkin' and whatever I think come right out. We didn't want you ever to know. You set such store by that boy, we wanted all your memories to be sweet."

165

Up to now, mostly what he'd remembered had been all tied up with those last days, memories anything but sweet: how his friend was suddenly gone, locked up in a box like he'd been bad, and how lost he'd felt when his mama and daddy had said no, he couldn't see Benjamin anymore. Sharp as yesterday he recalled how it had scared him when the grownups whispered in shocked tones, then hushed when he came around. That, and the hot day in the colored church, him and his parents sitting on the front row, and the steady swing of pasteboard fans as the solemn people sang of sweet home and bye 'n' bye's, and the sick feeling he got at seeing grown folks cryin', and him wondering why Benjamin had gone off and left him. That mournful music and the smell of Cape jasmines still filled his head whenever he thought of Benjamin. He looked up into Lily's worried eyes and swallowed to loosen his throat. "How come he burned?"

Her face drawn, she said, "My baby wont but six, he didn't know no better. He just got in the way."

"Daddy said the Klan didn't mean to kill him."

She looked at him sharp. "But they was out to harm, Bubba. Ole white men dressed up in sheets, like that made 'em even whiter." She looked down at her open hands. "My boy's blood marked a stain on their souls only the good Lord can wash out, and they knows it. He just another pickaninny to them, but he my boy" — she hit her chest — "and he not just another child to me — he my onliest child." Bubba slipped his hand into hers.

166

"That night, when we sees that firelight comin' in the window and hears them voices outside, whisperin' like they up to no good, all we can thinks is what they doin' to our place and is they gone kill us. I seen them white robes and them torches and that cross just a burnin' in the middle of my manure pile what Israel had brought round that very day for my garden.

"Israel and me, we don't say nothin', I just grabs up Benjamin, and runs out the back while he goes out the front. I puts my boy down a ways from the house, then I sneaks back. I ain't leavin' Israel to face them mens all by hisself. He up there standin' tall, askin' them whyfor they wants to burn a cross at his place."

Bubba kept his gaze on the grass while she talked. He could see it all in his mind's eye.

"And some man," she went on, "he step out and say, 'We don't want no uppity niggers livin' round here,' and it like poison comin' out his mouth. I'm fearin' for Israel, they lookin' so hateful. What they want all them firebrands for, they got that cross already burnin' so it's lightin' up the night? Then Mist Jed come runnin'."

Bubba looked up. Her eyes stared into the past.

"And he walks past me with his face set like a stone and steps up right aside of Israel. He say to them men, 'What business you got here?' And somebody say ain't none of his business. But Mist Jed, he stand his ground and say, 'Israel Wade business *is* my business. You hurt him, you got to answer to me.'" She stopped to take a breath. "Well, that man up in front kinda shuffled his feets around, then he say, 'We not out to harm. Just wants this nigger gone from these parts.' And Mist Jed, he pulled himself up straight and he say, 'Israel Wade ain't no nigger. He as good a colored as God ever made. Don't take no brown skin to make trash. Trash come in all colors, even them with yellow streaks up their backs, and ain't no white robe can hide that.' "

Bubba's eyes widened. "What'd that man do?"

"Well, he jump like he been slapped, and them others starts backin' off. 'I were you, men,' Mist Jed says, 'I'd take them robes home and burn 'em. This ain't a night's work to be proud of. Ain't no decent white man gone find fault with Israel here.'

"Now they starts actin' like they ready to call it a night, but that one man, he mad as all get-out, and he standin' his ground." She swallowed and took a deep breath, like she couldn't get enough air. Bubba squeezed her hand. "And right then, just right that minute, here come Benjamin, headin' lickety-split for his daddy, and he gone past 'fore I could grab the tail of his nightshirt. Right that same minute, that man, he liftin' his arm and throwin' that firebrand at the house, and it went up, up, and came down so slow and it headin' straight for my boy. My feets stuck to the ground and my voice stopped up, and then that burnin' pitch lands right on my baby and he on fire, he flame right up, and he's screamin', and I'm screamin' and runnin', and I falls. Israel and your daddy, they runnin', and we roll our boy over and over, tryin' to get that fire out, but that kerosene done soaked him and it too late. Too late." She held her arms and rocked. "And when we looks up, every one of them men gone like haints, and it's just me and Israel and my poor burned baby and your daddy, and that ole cross smolderin' down." The tears left silent trails on her cheeks.

Bubba was crying, too, and she lifted his chin with her finger and looked straight in his eyes. "And you knows, that cross the first thing I see? And I'm glad. They meant it for hate, but it mean love to me, and I fling out my arms and all I can say is 'Thank you, Jesus, thank you, Jesus, that my baby's pain is over and he didn't suffer no longer'n he did.' " She dropped her hands to her lap and sat quiet. Bubba blinked away the shimmer and waited.

When she went on, her voice came so soft he could hardly hear it. "Your daddy took off'n his shirt and wrapped my baby up in it so's I couldn't see no more, and he carried him in the house. Then he went to fetch your mama 'cause he knows Miss Ruby what I needs most right then. Your mama, she washed my Benjamin and doctored me and kissed my tears, and her gettin' heavy with child herself." She wiped her cheeks with the heel of her hand, and her voice got hard. "But ain't no tears ever washed away from my eyes the sight of that man throwing that brand, his robes aswirlin' in the firelight, and it archin' end over end and comin' down on my child."

They sat silent a long while. Finally Bubba sniffed and pinched his nose. "Do you know who it was?"

"Don't matter now. My boy just as dead. That man, he burnin' in his own hell, he don't need me to wish it for him. Hate do that to me, too, I let it."

Bubba looked down and without a word started picking the violets. As he lay them on Benjamin's grave, Lily's arm went around him. "That right nice of you, Bubba. Benjamin like that, I know. He like to know his ole friend remember him." His throat was too full to answer, but Lily went on. "Israel wanted everything in the world for that boy, he full of dreams, but that wont to be. All we can give him now is our love and rememberin'. That way, he still alive to us."

"I ain't never gone forget," he said.

"I 'preciates that." She nodded, "I tells you, Bubba, Benjamin child of my body and my heart, but you child of my heart, too. And that ain't no disloyalty to my boy. He love you like a brother." She shook her head like she was throwing off her mood and smiled, "And wouldn't he have somethin' to say, he see us standin' here and cryin'? Wouldn't like that atall. Most likely be sayin', 'Come on, Bubba, let's go get them dandelions for supper.' And he be comin' home with his hands full for me, and you with yourn for your mama."

"I can get some for you, too," Bubba whispered.

She smiled, "Now wouldn't that be fine? I tell you what, you help me finish up here, and we'll go find that patch together and pick us a pile. Then when Israel eats his greens tonight, I tell him they come from Benjamin, and won't he be surprised?"

He didn't want to get them for Israel — he wanted them for her — but he swallowed the words and nodded.

19

As they broke up the land for planting, the wind stirred whirls of dust that gritted Bubba's teeth. Israel's mule flicked its stub of a tail as Bubba tried to guide the plow so the rows would be straight and true. Across the field, Jed and Israel were spreading manure on the fallow land yet to be cut. Better this dust than that, Bubba thought, and wrinkled his nose. He'd stayed home from school to help out, but his mama had insisted that Scooter go. The boy hadn't been acting right lately, and Bubba didn't like the idea of Scoot being at school without him there. Uneasy, he scanned the sky. Blue as a robin's egg, and white clouds stringing across from the wind. He rubbed his neck and made a face at the roll of dirt that came off on his hand. Pig dirt. Mama'll have a fit.

His father halloed and waved toward the house.

Bubba signaled he'd come on, so the men headed back for dinner. He clucked at the mule, eager to get home and clear his throat with some cool ice tea. At the end of the row, he laid the reins across a bush and gratefully pulled in a lungful of fresh, clean air and the fragrance of new-turned earth. Spring coming. His mama's daffodils be blooming soon.

A horn honked, and a dusty black Ford bounced down the lane. Goin' mighty fast, he thought. Then the horn blared again and again. Frightened, Bubba broke into a run just as Jed and Israel hurried from the barnyard.

Two people got out of the car. Bubba caught a glimpse of red hair as he stumbled across the soft plowed dirt. Then his daddy cried out and snatched open the rear car door. Bubba's breath came sharp in his throat now, his heart hammering with fear as he saw Jed bend down into the car. A dark feeling closed in, and then he knew before he saw, and there they were — his daddy carrying a small body across the yard and Ruby running out to meet him, Israel following with the man and the girl.

It was Thora and Mr. Tetley. And Scooter.

Panting, he ran up into the yard past them, past Israel's restraining hand, and on into his mama's room. His daddy was laying the boy down on the bed. Scooter, with blood trickling out his nose and ear, and one arm bent funny. Scooter, with his eye puffed closed, and one shoe and sock gone. Bubba couldn't look away from the white naked foot. His mama bent over like the pain was in her, and Jed's hands clenched tight.

Bubba heard the truck start up and knew Israel was going for Lily. At his mama's look, he headed for the kitchen to get water and a towel. He'd thought Scooter was dead, like Benjamin, and the black moment had yawned out before him, till he'd heard him whimper. He hurried down the porch, not even really seeing the man and girl waiting at the foot of the steps.

Dinner was on the table, just like the day Scoot had almost drowned. This time wont nobody to blame but himself. He hadn't gone to school today, had left Scoot open to harm.

When he got back, they'd gotten Scooter's clothes off. Bruises stained the white skin, and his arm crooked at an angle that made Bubba's stomach turn over. With a nod, his mama dismissed him as she gently went to work.

Through the screen door, he saw his father and Mr. Tetley talking in low voices. Thora's face was bruised and dirty, and the bow in her hair hung loose. He blinked. Thora and Scooter both?

Jed was asking, "You telling me he didn't do a thing to stop it?" Tetley shook his head. "Just stood there and watched?"

Bubba could see the fury going up his daddy's back

and he walked out on the porch. Mr. Tetley's eyes looked sad, and Thora wouldn't look at him. He drew himself up. "What happened to Scooter?"

"He got in a fight, Bubba. Some of the older boys were picking on him, and Scooter just lit into them." Mr. Tetley shook his head. "Almost like they'd been waiting for him to."

"And they fought back?" Bubba asked. He looked at Thora digging a hole in the dirt with her toe, and then back again at Mr. Tetley. "Who?"

But it was Thora who answered, her voice a whisper. "It was Grady and Jarvis, Bubba. And Jimmy Leon." She flushed.

Jimmy Leon had claimed to be his friend.

"You sayin' *three* big boys ganged up on my boy?" Jed said. She nodded.

"Seems they've been giving Scooter a hard time all along," Mr. Tetley explained. "The whole thing just blew up today."

"Scooter never said nothin' to us about such."

"Pride, Mr. Harkins. Both your boys like to fend for themselves."

"All things being equal, I 'spect them to. But three older boys against one first-grader ain't what I call equal. Thought Scooter had more sense than that."

"He does, but they've been egging him on all winter."

"Somebody eggin' *them* on," Thora murmured.

Bubba felt sorry for her. It had taken a lot of guts for

her to come, knowing her brother was the ringleader of it all. "Grady gettin' back at me?"

She shook her head. "Ole Raggey."

"What you mean, girl?" Jed said.

"He's been actin' like Grady and them were special, lettin' 'em slide on their work, and all the time havin' somethin' to say about the Harkinses."

"Like what?" Jed's voice was sharp.

She looked down at the ground again.

"Best you tell him, Thora," Mr. Tetley said.

Her eyes went straight to Bubba as if begging his pardon for what she was about to say. "Tellin' 'em how Mr. Harkins done been in jail for moonshinin', and how he left you all to fend for yourselves, and how you're nothin' but niggerlovers." She said it fast and fixed her eyes on her feet again before Bubba could react.

Bubba's ears rang. He wished he had his hands round Ole Raggey's neck. He'd choke him good.

Jed sucked in a deep breath. "Niggerlovers?"

"That's what set Scooter off," Tetley said.

Thora spoke up. "You see, he was talkin' bout Israel and you havin' a snowball fight, and that's when Grady said it. And next thing I knew, Scooter was tearin' into him, yellin' for him to take it back, that Israel wont no nigger, and the other boys were laughin' and pullin' him off, but then he started hittin' them and it wont so funny anymore. They got Scooter down and were layin' into him and Ole Raggey just stood there in the door watchin'. I tried, but I couldn't get them off. Finally,

Mr. Tetley came and broke it up. Then he put Scooter in his car and we brought him home."

"She wanted to come with me," Tetley added.

Jed blinked, and his voice sounded tight. "Mighty beholden to you, Mr. Tetley. And to you, Miss Thora. 'Preciate you all tryin' to watch out for my boy."

Bubba's throat felt so full he couldn't speak. He kept seeing Scooter's beaten face. All that for nothin', 'cause Israel wont worth fightin' over.

Tetley ran his tongue across his lips. "No thanks needed, Mr. Harkins. Should have done something a long time ago." His shoulders squared. "I think we need to have a talk, once you have your boy squared away."

Jed's eyes narrowed. "No time like the present. Ruby'll call me if she needs me. Bubba, why don't you take Thora round back where she can wash herself up some, and then Mr. Tetley can take her back to school."

Bubba headed around the house, but when he realized Thora wasn't following, he came back and led her. Her palm felt soft against his. A flush burning his ears, he dropped her hand to point at the pump and basin on the side porch. "Help yourself." He waited on the steps while she splashed water on her face. "You know I'm gone have to get Grady," he said.

Thora stopped fixing her hair. " 'Spect so. He deserves a whippin'."

He studied the dusty tops of his shoes. "Thora, we

176

ain't no niggerlovers." He cleared his throat. "Israel and Lily is decent colored folk, they ain't niggers." Her eyes were straight on him now, waiting. "They helped us out a lot when we needed it, and Israel and my daddy grew up together, like you and me, and they just don't see no color. All they see is Israel and Jed. Mama and Lily, they're the same way." She didn't understand, and he was at a loss. He couldn't explain without saying they were friends, but he couldn't say that anymore because of Israel.

He went over to the pump. Once he got a strong stream of water going, he stuck his head under it. The cool water sluiced against his neck as he rubbed the itchy dirt and sweat away. The towel muffled the sound of Thora's voice. "What you say?" he asked.

Her voice was soft. "I said, do you love 'em?"

He studied the cloth. His mama'd have somethin' to say about all that dirt on her clean towel. He felt Thora waiting, and thought again about Israel. "Naw," he said. At that moment, the truck rattled into the yard. The doors slammed, and he knew Lily had come to take care of Scooter. His heart felt torn in two. He looked at Thora. Her eyes were sad, and he could tell she knew he hadn't spoken true.

When Bubba and Thora came back to the front of the house, they saw the men gathered under the chinaberry tree, their faces serious. Jed nodded at something Tetley said, then shook his hand, and the teacher

177

headed for the car, gesturing for Thora to follow. They got in and backed off in a cloud of dust.

Bubba walked closer to the men. His father and Israel had hunkered down beside the tree. "You reckon what he says is true?" Jed asked.

"Mist Tetley a good man. He don't lie."

"Didn't know a man could carry a hate like that." The pungent odor of a wild onion sprout drifted on the air as Jed tore its strands. "I never gave him cause."

"I knows that, and you knows that. But he don't think like you and me, he think like hisself." Israel paused. " 'Spect his thinkin' been twisted some, what with the war and all."

Raggey. They were talking about Ole Raggey.

"But he's takin' his spite out on my boys."

"Can't get to you, got to take it out on somebody. 'Sides, he get one of yourn, he get you." They fell silent. Bubba tried to ignore an ant crawling up his arm. He didn't want to move. Israel went on, "You think Mist Tetley really gone talk to the school board?"

"Won't do no good. My daddy did the same thing."

"Huh. Ole Raggey Young Raggey then, and he a hero from the war. Things is different now. He know he been goin' too far, that why he let them boys do his dirty work. He sly."

"I should have give him whatfor when he laid his first hand on Bubba."

"Huh. That woulda pleased him just fine. He'd

aknowed he hurt you." He put his hand on Jed's arm. "Thing for you now is to have a care. He dast not touch your boys again, but he gone try somepin' else, sure as I live."

From where he stood, Bubba could see Israel's dark hand on Jed's arm. He wanted to knock the hand away, wanted to cry out a warning not to trust him. Jed took a deep breath and stood, brushing the grass from his pants. "It's a hard thing to know someone wishes you ill, but I'm glad Tetley told me."

"Jed?" Ruby was at the door. "We need your help."

"Coming," he answered, and went to the house.

Israel watched him go. "Bubba, that one fine man."

Bubba met his eye. "You should know." Israel nodded, and sitting on the edge of the porch, leaned back against a post. "What was all that talk about Ole Raggey? He mean my daddy harm?"

"Your daddy a grown man, he can look out for his-self." Israel slid his hat down over his eyes.

Bubba's resentment welled, but before he could speak, a sharp cry came from the house, then another. The sound hung on the still afternoon air, then fell to whimpers. Bubba already had his hand on the door when Israel said, "Settin' his arm. Worst over now."

Mr. Tetley's Ford pulled into the yard again, this time with Doc Swinson's Cadillac following. The doctor got out with his bag and went on in the house. Tetley came over. Israel stood. "Thought it best I get him," the teacher explained.

Israel nodded. "They just set his arm."

"That ear didn't look right to me either."

Bubba bit his lip. " 'Preciate you thinkin' bout it, Mr. Tetley. Scooter's arm looked so bad, I doubt anybody thought much bout his ear." But he should have; he'd seen the blood coming out of it.

Tetley looked at him sharp. "Don't you go blaming yourself for all this, Bubba. The fault lies somewhere else. Like I told Ira Swinson, he and Raggenbotham may have been friends a long time, but there's a limit to making excuses for anybody. Something should have been said before this. That was my error."

"Ain't your fault, Mist Tetley. Everybody knows you a good man."

"But 'the only thing necessary for evil to flourish is for good men to do nothing,' " Tetley quoted softly. "Remember, Bubba?" Bubba didn't, but he nodded anyway. "History lesson, son. History is truth, and it's past time for truth. At one time, the Klan did their best to scare Israel away from these parts." Bubba knew all that and wished Mr. Tetley wouldn't say anymore. He didn't want to think about Benjamin now, with Scooter so hurt. "But your father stood up for what was right against his friends and neighbors," Tetley went on, "and that night pretty well put an end to the Klan in this area. That shows what one good man can do, and the harm wrong-thinking men can do. And you saw that again today." The teacher's intent eyes made Bubba feel that Mr. Tetley was trying to tell him something, but making him think of the answer himself, like he did at school. Then Tetley put his hand on Israel's shoulder and said, "For whatever good it does for one white man to say it, Israel, I'm sorry."

"Wont none of your doin', Mist Tetley."

Suddenly Bubba wondered if Ole Raggey had had something to do with the Klan. He felt proud his daddy had stood up to them.

When Doc Swinson came out with Jed, his eyes were flat with anger. "Didn't want to worry Ruby, but that ear doesn't look good," he said in an undertone. "Might have some hearing loss." Jed nodded, his lips tight. The doctor cleared his throat. "I'm bound to say I'm sorry as I can be, Jed. Wouldn't have had something like this happen for the world." He extended his hand.

Jed took it. "I 'preciate you comin' out so quick."

"Anytime. Anytime. I'll be by to check him again tomorrow. And no charge, mind." He held up his hand as Jed started to protest. "Someone else will pay, I guarantee you that. Someone else will pay," he repeated as he got in his car.

"I'd best get back to school," Tetley said. "I hope Scooter heals well, Mr. Harkins. Let me know if there's anything else I can do."

"Can't thank you enough for what you already done."

"It was nothing. Nothing," Tetley shook his head.

No one spoke as the two cars pulled away. Then

Bubba's worry spilled out. "Did Doc mean Scooter ain't gone be able to hear no more?"

"Just maybe in that one ear."

"But he still got one good one, Bubba," Israel said. "Thank the Lord for that."

Thank the Lord for what? he thought. He turned on his heel and headed across the yard.

The side of the barn gave some shelter from the cool wind as he sat next to Queen's grave. He pulled his knees up and rested his head on his arms. Even if he shut his eyes, he could still hear Scooter's gut cry, still see that white foot and the blood on his mama's good pillowcase. Scoot hadn't had a chance against them big boys. Ole Raggey had no call to let him get hurt, nor Grady to take out his spite on a little kid.

He leaned his head against the sun-warmed side of the barn. For the first time, he felt whipped. His brother lay in there beat to pieces, maybe goin' deaf, his mama's heart was breakin', and the daddy that had come back didn't seem like his daddy at all. And his friend Israel had turned out to be no friend, and Queen was dead.

20

Bubba waited in the trees near the sawmill to catch Grady on his way home from school. Somebody was gone pay for his mama's tears and Scooter's hurt. Behind him, the big blades squealed as each log went in, spewing sawdust onto a mountainous pile, sweetening the air with the smell of new-cut wood. As the wailing saws stopped, he heard voices, and saw them coming, Grady and Jarvis and Jimmy Leon. Thora trailed along behind, her bow still crooked, her bruised cheek turning purple now.

He stepped out into the road. "Grady Ferrell."

"What you want?" Grady asked, startled. The other boys closed up behind him, but Thora stood apart.

"Want your hide," Bubba said. Grady stepped back nearer his friends. Jarvis smirked, but Jimmy Leon cut his eyes away from Bubba. "You picked on the wrong one this time, Grady. Scooter's my brother, and now you got to deal with me." When Grady still didn't move, Bubba threw his taunt: "Ain't nothin' but a low-down chickensnake pick on a little kid."

"I ain't no chickensnake!"

"Maybe you just chicken."

Grady looked at the other boys, but they had backed away. "You ain't gone fight all three of us?"

"You watch me try."

Grady turned to the others, laughing. "Hey, you reckon he's got his nigger friends hidin' in them woods?" Jarvis snickered, then Jimmy Leon joined in.

Bubba's voice came out in a soft hiss. "They ain't got no time to mess with white trash like you."

"Who you callin' white trash?"

"Who you callin' niggerlover?"

"Who you callin' chickensnake?"

"That chicken what's standin' right there, won't come fight."

"Come on then!" Dropping his lunch pail and book bag, Grady bent his knees and put his hands up.

They circled each other, then Grady's fist flicked out. Bubba's right hand knocked it aside while his left went straight for Grady's cheek. As the boy struck back, Bubba backed off, and Grady's arm fanned the air. Grinning, Bubba closed in again, but Grady jumped back out of range, hollering, "Come on, you guys, let's get him!" The other two boys exchanged glances while Bubba stood panting, both fists still up.

"I'd stay put if it was me," Thora said. "This is 'tween him and Grady."

"Yeah, Grady, you ought to be able to handle him by yourself," Jimmy Leon said. Jarvis nodded.

Grady's jaw dropped. Bubba jumped him, and they went down into the dirt, rolling into the sawdust. The shriek of the saws all but drowned out their grunts. Then Grady was on top, punching solid hits. Bubba threw him off. The boy scrambled to his feet and bolted to the sawdust pile. His sliding feet sent rivulets of sawdust down the sides as he pumped his legs to climb higher. Right behind him, Bubba grabbed his shirt neck, and both fell into the dry sawdust, thrashing their way down into the wet powder below. Bubba spat and shook his head, sending sawdust flying. He rubbed a handful in Grady's face. Choking, the boy tried to wipe his eyes, one hand still flinging wild blows.

Now Bubba had him down. They rolled again, and Grady was on top. Bubba heard men shouting, but then he was straddling Grady again and saw only his red rage and Grady's head pillowed on the sawdust, mouth slack and the blood running. Bubba hit again and again. One for Scooter. One for Mama. One for Thora. One for Lily. One for Benjamin . . . Then somebody was on him, kicking. Sharp nails tore at his hair, fists beat on his back. "Leave him be! Leave him be!" Thora screamed.

The fight went out of him then, and he rolled off Grady. Her green eyes sparking, Thora tried to keep her balance on the sliding dust. "Ain't no call to beat the life out of him!" she cried, tears tracking through the yellow grit on her cheeks. He looked at Grady, eyes crusted, blood dribbling from his nose and clotting into sawdust clumps, and felt ashamed.

"What you kids doing up there? You come down right now!" A bandy-legged sawmill worker stood at the bottom, his hands on his hips. Thora pulled at Grady's hand, but he couldn't get up. Bubba struggled to his feet and plowed over to help. Between them, he and Thora carried him down the pile, breaking their slide with their heels.

Jarvis and Jimmy Leon were gone. Only the mill worker stood there. "Kids," the man said, shaking his head. He saw Grady feebly trying to clear his mouth as Thora wiped at the sawdust on his eyes. He went and got a bucket of water, tilting it high over Grady's head. The boy cried out and spat a wad of sawdust. "That better?" the man asked, grinning. Grady nodded, his eyes down and hair dripping.

"Thanks," Thora said.

"Reckon you can get him home, little lady?"

She nodded. "You can walk, can't you, Grady?"

He wiped his hand across his swollen lips and mumbled, "That nigger sure taught you how to fight."

Bubba stopped shaking the sawdust out of his shoe.

"Ain't your mouth got you in enough trouble for one day, Grady Ferrell?" Thora said. "You deserved that beatin'. If you wont my brother, I'da let him kept on." She stomped over to pick up their pails and bags.

The shoe still in his hand, Bubba watched them go. His cheek throbbed, his hands hurt, and he itched from the grit in his clothes, and what good had it done? Scooter was still hurt, and beating up Grady hadn't brought his hearin' back. Bubba's spent anger left a bitter taste in his mouth.

He made his way home barefoot, carrying his shoes. When he got to the lane that led to Israel's, he hesitated. It'd save scarin' his mama half to death if Lily'd help him get cleaned up first. Israel would be at his chores, so he wouldn't have to see him. He turned up the path. From the barn, he heard Israel singing, "Swing low, sweet chariot . . ." and his mind's eye saw again the tenants on the road the day Queen had died. Suddenly the picture changed, and Lily and Israel sat hunched on the wagon instead. Uneasy, he walked faster.

"My mercy, boy, ain't you a sight in this world? What's that you got all over you?" Lily said when she saw him.

"Sawdust."

"Huh." She got her broom from the kitchen. "You ain't comin' in my house trackin' that trash. Stand still now." She brushed him, knocking sawdust in the air. Her eyes narrowed at the sight of his bruises. "You been fightin'?" He nodded. She sighed, shaking her head. "I'll get you some of Israel's clothes. Come on in when you done rinsin' off."

Rolling up the sleeves on the oversized shirt, he hurried into the kitchen where Lily waited, towel and basin ready. She cupped his chin in her hand. "Hmph.

187

Face only a ma could love," she said in a familiar tease, "but she sure wouldn't like to see it now." He flinched as the soapy water stung his cheek like hot peppers. "You try to grind this mess down to the bone?"

"Grady did. I got him for beatin' up Scooter." He fell silent as she rinsed. He saw her black bag in the corner. "They're sayin' Scoot might lose some of his hearin'."

She nodded. "That ear hurt somewhat bad."

He kept quiet a minute, then blurted, "Seems like there been nothin' but trouble since *he* came back."

"Your daddy ain't had nothin' to do with it."

I ain't got no daddy, Bubba thought. My real daddy got gone the day he went off to prison. "Things ain't the same. *He* ain't the same," he said.

"Law, boy, neither are you," she laughed. "You favor your daddy so much, it a wonder you don't look twice in the mirror." He pulled back, but she shook her head. "Change don't matter, Bubba. That blood bond still there, and the love the same. Why, ain't a day go by I don't love my Benjamin, and he been dead these nigh on seven years." Her voice softened, "Your daddy's love still there, too. Same as with me and Israel. We loves you like our own, and nothin' gone change that."

Bubba saw the concern in her face and felt pulled toward her like when he was little and would fling himself in her arms. But he was most grown now, and

188

he wouldn't. There were things Lily didn't know. Things he wished he didn't know.

21

Still aching from the fight, Bubba attacked the sprouting weeds with his hoe as they got the garden ready for the Good Friday planting. Another cold snap had hit, and he rubbed his hands together to get them warm. If it weren't for the woods looking like a hazy green patchwork, he'd have doubted spring would ever be here. In her calico poke bonnet, his mama was working the garden row ahead of him, humming softly. Farther down, Jed spread the henhouse droppings. As the two called back and forth to each other, Bubba looked away. He was glad to see his mama laugh, but Lordy, they got enough troubles without his father makin' jokes. His hoe sliced a worm neatly in two as his mind ran on. Scooter with his arm broke and only half able to hear. Money short and plantin' time coming up. He brought the hoe down again. No crops this year, there wont no way to get by next. No way to pay taxes neither. And they standing out here talkin' bout beans like they wont no danger of hard times or losing this place.

They caught his attention again when Jed said, "Ruby, I been thinkin'." She stopped hoeing. He kept shoveling the guano, not looking at her. "Bout gettin' some work over to Roanoke Rapids at the mill."

Her head jerked back. "Whyfor?" Bubba stopped hoeing and listened.

Jed wiped his arm across his forehead, then saw the expression on her face. "Now Ruby, don't you go gettin' upset. This be just temporary, to set some money by. Why, with this new law, I can get two dollars a day, and gettin' this place built up again gone take money for seed, for mules, for taxes."

"But what about the plantin'?" she said. "Growin' season's comin', and the land don't wait."

"It'll get done," Jed said. "Fields are ready, and I'll be home weekends. Israel will help."

Bubba turned his hoe a circle in the soft dirt, excited. It would be just him and his mama and Scooter again, like it used to be, 'cept on the weekends. His hoe stilled. Naw, it wouldn't either, 'cause Israel had always been there to help before, and he didn't want no help from him. He rubbed his hands on his pants, then started working again.

A dust curl traveled up the road, and Israel's truck pulled in, the horn beeping. His parents exchanged questioning looks as they headed for the truck, Ruby wiping her hands on her apron. Bubba didn't care about seeing Israel — he wished he wouldn't come around at all. He chopped a clod of earth so hard the pieces went flying. Then he saw Israel and Lily both get out of the truck. Somethin' must be up for her to come in the middle of the day, he thought. Curious, he went over, trying to make his walk casual.

But they were only talking. He shifted from one foot to the other, feeling foolish. Then he thought he saw something move in Israel's pocket. Nobody said anything. Maybe he hadn't seen it. But then there it was again. What you reckon he's got in that pocket?

They looked at him. "Well, reckon that's for me to know and you and Scoot to find out," Israel said with a wink at Jed, and led the way to the house. Bubba hadn't meant to say it out loud, and most of all he didn't like grown-up secrets. But he followed them anyway.

Turned out it was a puppy. A black squirmtail puppy that crawled up Scooter's lap and made him laugh. The boy had been quiet of late and not himself. He was healing slow, and it hurt Bubba each time he saw him favor his left ear to hear better. But his brother's excitement over the puppy brought pink back to his cheeks. Bubba was glad, even though an old pain roused when the wiggling puppy licked Scooter under his chin. Bubba felt Israel's eyes on him.

"You gone have to share this here puppy, Scooter," Israel said. "Like Bubba and your daddy shared Queen."

"Oh, I will. We'll teach it to hunt and fetch and everything. Won't we, Bubba? Soon's I get better."

191

Bubba nodded. The puppy wriggled, pushing back the blanket on Scooter's legs, and then it started gnawing on his cast. "And it'll almost be like Queen being back. We can even call her Queenie."

"No," Bubba said, and the boy's face fell.

"There can't ever be but one Queen, son," Jed said. "You can think of another name."

"That's right," Israel agreed. "Each dog his own special self, and he entitled to his own special name."

"*Her* name," Lily said. "It a girl dog, like Queen."

"But she ain't Queen. She's her own self, and she got to have a name," Scooter said.

"How bout we name her after that queen in the Bible story?" Ruby said. "The queen of Sheba."

"That's it." Scooter nodded hard. "We can call her Sheba. That all right with you, Bubba?" Bubba nodded. "Now she got her own name!" He stopped in surprise. "Uh oh," he said, and they all laughed as Ruby scooped up the dripping puppy.

"Look like some trainin' got to be done quick."

"Got your work cut out, Scoot," Bubba said. "I'll help. Leastways till you get that cast off."

Now what did I say a fool thing like that for? Bubba wondered as the puppy tumbled around the yard on its short legs. The cold wind blew straight out of the gray sky, but Sheba only wanted to sniff around.

"Hurry up, dog. Do your stuff." It nosed around a

shriveled chinaberry. "Aw, that's it," Bubba grumbled, kneeling to scoop it out of her mouth.

Do seem like Israel could have found a dog wont so dumb. He noticed the puppy shivering, squinting its eyes against the wind. He picked her up. "Now don't you go doing your mess on me," he warned as he pulled his sweater around her. Soon the shivering stopped, and the puppy nuzzled up to lick his neck. Stroking her ear, he held her closer, letting the soft body ease the cold stone in his chest.

"Dog ain't never gone get housebroke like that," Israel's voice came from the porch.

"She started shiverin'. Won't do no good for her to get sick." Bubba put the puppy down. Reluctantly he said, "Have to say I 'preciate you bringin' this here puppy to Scooter."

"Glad to do it. Everybody needs somepin' to love, takes 'em out of theirselves." He cocked his head. "I ever tell you bout the turtle?"

"What's a turtle got to do with anything?"

The big man ignored his sharp tone. "Ole turtle go along fine till trouble come, then he pull back into that shell of his'n. Sure enough, he don't get hurt that way, but problem is, they's only room in that shell for one. Dark in there. Lonesome, too," he added.

"So?"

"Man ain't meant to be no turtle, Bubba. He needs friends and love and light. Ain't no call to shut hisself off, but it's up to him." Israel touched his shoulder. "Sure am missin' my young buddy. Your daddy hurtin' for you, too." Bubba studied the ground. "Leave go, Bubba. Whatever it is you holdin' in so tight hurtin' us, but hurtin' you most of all. Leave go," he repeated, then he turned and left.

School would be out in a couple of weeks, and Bubba could hardly wait. He didn't like looking at Grady's bruised face, and Raggey stayed sour as a green apple. But he and Thora had gotten to be friends, and when he told her about the Wades bringing the puppy, he finally admitted that he'd told her a lie, and all she said was, "Shucks, Bubba, I know you love 'em — it's writ all over you. Be hard put not to love folks like that."

Well, he did love Lily, so he didn't correct her. "I guess that makes us niggerlovers."

"Friends is friends." Her voice turned wistful. "Wish I had me some friends like that."

"You got a friend," he said, and reddened.

"You got me, too, I reckon. 'Ceptin' when you start beatin' up on my brother."

Relieved she'd made a joke of it, he laughed. They were dawdling going in after recess. Ole Raggey wasn't at school, gone to Allton on business. Buying up more land, Bubba guessed.

"What's he want all that land for anyway?" Thora

194

said. "Seems like he takes advantage of people's hard times. I wouldn't want nothing I got like that."

Bubba could hardly see her freckles, her cheeks were so pink. "Me neither," he agreed.

"My daddy says the school board is so fired up about Scooter, they might get rid of him." At the schoolhouse door, she stopped and ran her hand along the door frame. "Wish we could stay here next year. That new high school's got people from all over the county, people we don't even know. It's scary."

"Naw. At least we get to ride the bus every day." He looked around, then slipped his hand into hers. It felt small and fragile in his, like a bird. "Don't worry, I'll look out for you."

"You will?"

"Sure," he said, then cleared his throat as he put his hand back in his pocket. "Ain't friends got to stick by one another?"

She smiled and went on inside. He had a sudden urge to pull her long sash but just grinned instead.

It was drizzling as he hurried home, but he didn't feel it. White dogwood blossoms peeped out from the greening trees, and the honeysuckle azaleas glowed pink, releasing their sweet smell on the air. It wasn't until he broke off a branch of dogwood for Scooter that he realized he'd been whistling.

Israel's truck was parked under the chinaberry tree.

Bubba threw his book bag on the porch and went straight into the kitchen. Israel and Jed sat across from each other, coffee cups in their hands. Bubba opened the safe and pulled out the remains of an apple pie and a sweet potato. As he peeled the potato, Jed said, "You want some coffee with that?"

"Umph," Bubba nodded, his mouth stuffed.

Jed poured him a cup. "Here, sit down. Unless you don't want to get too far from more food," he added.

Bubba realized he had his fork already digging into the pie and looked up. The men were grinning. His face got hot as Israel laughed, "Growin' boy there. Eat you out of house and home, you ain't careful."

"Somethin' sure perked up his appetite. Haven't seen him eat like that in I don't know when," Jed said.

Bubba curled his hands around the warm cup and said, "Ole Raggey wont at school today. Mr. Tetley said he gone to the county seat on business."

The two men looked at each other. "I ain't too sure I like the sound of that," Jed said.

Israel nodded. "When that man make a move, most times trouble close behind. He love land like the Devil love evil. Well, Allton welcome to him. Better trouble there than trouble here."

"I don't know. After what Tetley told us, I just as soon have him where I can keep an eye on him."

Israel put his cup down. "You right," he said, his

face solemn. "That man got a grudge he won't forget. Best we don't forget neither."

Jed nodded and fell silent. Bubba looked down at his pie. His appetite was gone.

22

The sun was shining for the first time in a week as Bubba gathered up the garden tools. Clouds were building in the west and he had a feeling the sun wouldn't last long, but his mama was determined to put in the garden on Good Friday as usual, whether his father was here or not.

Jed had gone to Roanoke Rapids looking for work. After talking with Israel when Ole Raggey had gone to Allton, he'd been restless, then two days ago he'd left. His mama hadn't liked it, but Bubba had been relieved, at first. But it turned out to be not like the old times at all. He'd never known two days could be so long. He was always expecting to hear his father's whistle coming from the barn, and the house seemed empty.

"Bubba, you got spring fever? Bring them tools, this garden ain't made for waitin'," Ruby said.

She'd put a bench in front of Scooter and had him sorting out seeds, his cast shining white in the sun. Looks like a little old man, Bubba thought, with his mama's scarf wrapped tight around his head and a blanket over his lap. But at least he was outside. The puppy saw Bubba and scrambled over the ridges of dirt, its tail wagging. Bubba smiled, his mood lifting.

"You get them seeds ready, Scooter. We're gone be ready to put 'em in the ground in a minute," Ruby called as she took the hoe and picked her way across the soft soil, the puppy dodging under her feet until she almost tripped. "Land I pray, that dog's gone be the death of me yet," she said, and scooped her up. "Ought to throw her to the hogs. Sorry thing ain't good for nothing 'cept messin' my floors." She started toward the hogpen.

Scooter reached out, hollering, "No, Mama, don't you give Sheba to no hogs! Mama!"

She came back, her bonnet flipping to hang down by its strings, and plopped the puppy down on Scooter's lap. "You watch her then. But don't let her do nothin' on my good blanket, you hear?"

Scooter tucked the dog between his legs. It looked up at him expectantly. "Now you be a good dog, Sheba," he said, wagging his finger. When he went back to sorting the seeds on the bench, Sheba put her head down on his thigh, her eyes following his every move.

"Now maybe we can get some work done," Ruby

said, pulling her bonnet forward, but not before Bubba saw the smile wrinkling her eyes.

When the afternoon air cooled, Scooter had been sent back inside. The boy'd stalled for time, and only when Ruby spoke sharp did he scurry to the house. Bubba hadn't liked the way he hung back. He'd been sticking closer than a burr lately, looking like a question was going to pop out any minute, but it hadn't. "You ready for those seeds you got soakin'?" he asked his mama.

Ruby wiped her blowing hair away from her eyes. "Best get them in, I 'spect. Be dark sooner'n I thought."

The kitchen felt stuffy after the fresh air. "Came to get those seeds we had soakin'," he said at Scooter's glad look. The boy gazed out the window again. "You want to talk about what's been eatin' you?"

Scooter's bottom lip paled as he tried to keep it still. "I don't wanna go back to school," he got out.

"Whyforever not? I thought you liked Mr. Tetley."

"I'm scared of Grady Ferrell," he whispered.

He should have known. "You got no call to worry bout Grady. He ain't gone bother you. I showed him already he best not."

"You did?" The relief in Scooter's eyes almost made the fight with Grady worth it, Bubba thought.

After supper, Ruby sent Bubba to her room for some salve, for Scooter had started a cough. "I shouldn't have let him sit outside," she said, "but it seemed so hard to keep him shut in on the first pretty day."

Her room felt uncomfortable to him now. It still smelled like her Cashmere Bouquet, and the wedding ring quilt and the picture of Jesus kneeling by the rock were the same, but in the light from the door he could see Jed's overalls hanging from a nail and his shave cup by the basin. Bubba cut his eyes away from the tumbled work boots by the bed and searched the dresser for the Vicks mentholatum jar. He found it tucked behind a wooden statue he'd never seen. He picked it up. It was of a small boy resting his hand on the head of the dog beside him.

His mama's shadow fell across the floor. "What's taking you so long, son? That salve was right there . . ."

He showed her the carving. "What's this?"

She took it, her eyes tender. "Your daddy did it while he was away. Said he used to look at it every night before he went to sleep." She held it up to the light. "Can't you tell? It's you and Queen."

He took it from her. The boy seemed mighty small compared to the dog. His back felt rubbed smooth. "He did this of me?"

She nodded, her smile widening. "I'm glad you've seen it. He's been shy about showing it to you."

"Don't look like me to me."

"Does to me. You hardly look like the same boy now." Her eyes sparkled, "Ain't near so cute."

He had to answer her smile as he put the statue

200

down. He followed her out, then turned for a last look at the carving in the dim light. That boy sure looked little. He couldn't believe he'd ever been that small.

Easter Sunday, and Jed, excited over getting a mill job, had agreed to go to church for the first time since Preacher Satterthwaite had turned his back on him at the store. As they came into the churchyard, Ruby's pleasure at having her whole family with her glowed out of her face. She'd crocheted a new white collar for her red dress and Bubba thought she looked fine as he'd ever seen her. The men were standing outside as usual, murmuring and working tobacco quids in their cheeks. Bubba lagged behind, dreading their stares, afraid they would coldshoulder his father again. He was wearing that suit from the prison and looked different from the others in their Sunday galluses and blue serge pants.

But everybody's eyes traveled to Scooter's white cast and locked there until Ruby urged him inside the double doors of the church with a hand at his back. His father stopped, leaving Bubba in a dilemma. By all rights, he should have gone on in with his mama. He wasn't old enough yet to be congregating with the men, but he felt reluctant to leave Jed alone. Off to the side, Mr. Tetley and Shade Fields were talking. The teacher was sure worked up about something, his hands hitting the air fast like he did at school, and the more he said, the sterner Shade Fields's face got. Then

Fields spotted them, and he and Tetley came over. "Mighty fine day, Mr. Harkins," Tetley said. "Glad to see you here."

Jed's shoulders relaxed. "Glad to see you, too."

The last bell rang. Spitting out their quids, the men trailed into the church. Mr. Tetley and Shade Fields followed with Jed. Bubba sighed, relieved.

The Ferrells came hurrying up. Thora had on a blue flowered dress that moved soft in the breeze and grown-up white patent leather shoes. Suddenly she wasn't the Thora he'd always known anymore, and he was sharply aware of his wool little-boy knickers.

"Happy Easter, Bubba. Ain't you comin' in?" At his nod, she grabbed his hand. "Well, come on then."

The heat went up his neck, and he jerked his hand back. He saw the hurt flick across her face. "I'm coming," he floundered. "Don't have to pull me in."

She swung her red hair. "All right then, smarty-pants. See if I care."

That sounded more like the old Thora, and he relaxed. "You lookin' too pretty and grown-up to be haulin' me around," he explained, and then it was her turn to flush. He took her arm and they hurried on inside just as the congregation sang, "Up from the grave He arose . . ."

He sat in the stuffy church wishing the sermon was over, trying to keep his mind off the itchy prickles from his wool pants. His father sat straight and tall on

202

the men's side, Ole Raggey just a few rows back with his eyes burning square on the back of Jed's head. Bubba watched until the man looked away.

Preacher Satterthwaite finally gave the invitation to come to the altar, and the choir swung into "Just As I Am," Mrs. Fields's nasal voice twanging above the rest. Bubba noticed the preacher staring hard at Jed. His father looked back and didn't move. Bubba smiled. Jed Harkins wont about to go down to the altar, always said once was good enough. 'Sides, it would be like admitting he'd done wrong.

After church, the women flocked around Ruby, patting Scooter on the head and asking about him like he wasn't even there. The boy looked at Bubba for mercy, so he took him over to Jed.

"You all right, son?"

"Like to got a crick in my neck from them ole women," Scooter complained.

"Well, I like to got a crick in my backside on that bench. Seems to me they could get some cushions."

"You got to grow your own," said Ray Foster as he came up. "My Hilda bout fed me till I don't even feel that hard seat. You tell Ruby to fatten you up some."

"She tries, she tries," Jed said, grinning.

Foster's face turned serious. "Mighty sorry to hear about your trouble."

"I thank you."

"Seems like it don't rain but it pours. Your boy doing all right?"

"Doin' fair."

The man shook his head. "Sorry thing to do. Man ought to have a better care of children in his charge. Amongst other things." He gave Jed a meaning look.

Now Henry Howell joined them. "Heard what happened, Jed. Anything I can do?"

Jed looked puzzled. "Not that I know of."

"Well, you think of anything, you just let me know." And Howell and Foster walked away.

Jed's eyes followed them, then Ruby came up, flustered and pleased. "I swan, ain't everyone been nice today? I ain't never had so many people speak."

Something else was going on, and Bubba didn't know what. Like folks was saying one thing and meaning another. He didn't think his daddy understood either.

Then his mama said, "Mrs. Fields told me the school board is gone have a meetin'." She dropped her voice, "You reckon they gone let Mr. Raggenbotham go?" They looked over to where Raggey stood alone, then quickly looked away.

"No tellin'," Jed said.

Bubba remembered Ole Raggey's look at Jed in church. It reminded him how that muskrat had looked last winter in that trap. Like pure hate.

23

Bubba sat straight up in bed and stared into the lightening dark. His mind scrabbling for reality, he looked down at Scooter sleeping beside him. It was a wonder he hadn't waked him up, crying out and all.

The ragged edges of the nightmare still clung like a spiderweb. There had been the tenant wagon again, except this time he and his mama and Scoot had been on the wagon seat. Some sense of warning made him turn around, and he'd seen the creature. It had the body of a muskrat, but was ten times its size, and yellow hatin' eyes in a snake's head, and it was rarin' to strike. Bubba's hands had been tangled in the reins, and he could only stutter a warning "Puh puh puh," and that's when he woke up. Suddenly feeling shut in, he pulled on his overalls and slipped down the stairs.

The kitchen wing stood like a black block against the brightening sky as he stepped off the porch. He breathed in the cool air and swung himself up into the chinaberry tree, ignoring the cold drips from the early dew. He looked out at his world, needing to reassure himself it was all still there. Fog hung in the branches of the black woods around the fields as the rising sun etched the clouds with gold, and long shadows fell from the outbuildings. Clucking chickens and guinea hens came out to peck at the ground. He heard the soft tone of the clock as it struck six and recalled the times he'd lay in his bed hearing that clock whir and chime. When he was just a little thing, every morning when it sounded, he'd call downstairs to his mama, "Six-a-ma-clock, Bubba?" and his daddy would come upstairs laughing to carry him to their room on his shoulder. It had become a family joke, until finally the name had stuck, and he'd been Bubba from then on, not Jed Jr. anymore.

That clock was the sound of home, just like this tree had been here ever since he could remember, and the family graveyard on the hill. He recalled the coin in the chimney mortar his daddy had showed him long ago that his great-grandaddy had put there, and a fierce possessiveness grew inside him. This was their homeplace, owned free and clear. No landlord could make them leave. Having a dream didn't make it so.

He saw his mama go in the kitchen, and then Israel's truck pulled in. It stopped in a flurry of dust, and Israel looked out the window, grinning. "You up and at 'em right smart this morning, ain't you?"

Embarrassed at being caught in the tree again, Bubba didn't answer. As he climbed down, Israel got out and propped one foot on the running board. "What you doin' up there so early?" he asked.

"Nothin'," Bubba mumbled.

"Well, I reckon that's as good a place to be doing nothin' as they is," Israel said. "Come to see what all I can do to help out while your daddy at the mill."

"We're doin' fine," Bubba said, not looking at him.

"Mm hmm. Got me some extra seed corn here I can't use." Bubba was torn. They needed the seed bad. "Cat got your tongue, boy?"

His head came up then. "I ain't no boy."

Israel's eyes widened. "Well, excuse me," he said. "You want I should say 'young man,' or you want it 'sir'?"

Bubba swallowed. "Reckon you'll have to talk to my daddy about the corn. Can't take it without his say-so."

"You know good and well your daddy be glad to get that corn. He needin' all the help he can get."

"We can make our own help. He's feelin' beholden enough to you already, he says," Bubba blurted.

"Ain't no such thing as beholden 'tween friends. If they was, it's me standin' in your daddy's debt."

"I know," Bubba said, looking at him straight.

Israel's eyes flickered. "That's right. We been friends this long time. He been mighty good to me, and it pleases me to be good back when I can."

"You don't have to."

"Have-to ain't got nothin' to do with it."

"Might." He wished Israel would go home before he said something he shouldn't.

"Might what?"

"Might have somethin' to do with have-to."

"Boy, maybe you best spit out what you got to say."

"I'm saying we don't want your leavin's, and we don't need no help," Bubba snapped.

"That the way you want it, that the way you got it. My patience with you wore bout thin as it gone get." Israel got in the truck and slammed the door. "Eatin' pride makes a dry feast, Bubba. You remember that." And he was gone, the dust pluming from his wheels.

Ruby came out on the porch. "What did Israel go off so fast for? I was gone fix him a cup of coffee."

"Had some work to do," Bubba mumbled. "Said he'd be back later." The lie lay sour on his tongue.

"Well, I will be swan," she shook her head. "That man always so willin' to help. I don't know what we'd do without him, and that's the truth." As the door closed behind her, Bubba wished he could dig a hole and pull it in after. What'd he say that to Israel for? He knew full well they were gone have to have the man's help. Suddenly he felt the nightmare's shadow again, and he didn't know how he would ever face his father.

Friday, and Israel hadn't come back all that week. Bubba knew he was going to catch it from his father for talking the way he had, and he yearned for Monday and school, but then remembered school had let out. It would be just him and his daddy and Israel and the land all summer long.

Jed got home late that night and left the house early the next morning. Bubba heard the door click as he went out, going to get Israel. He lay there with the dread till he couldn't stand it anymore and got up. He hadn't slept much anyway, his thoughts darting first one way then another, like minnows in the creek. Even his dozing was full of dreams he couldn't remember, except they all left him with a bad feeling inside.

He'd slopped the pigs, chopped more wood, even fixed the door to the smokehouse before he saw his father coming back. He put down his hammer, relieved the time had finally come. Jed had a hard look as he marched across the yard. "You and me got to talk, boy," he said. Bubba followed him as he struck off toward the back field.

Once they were in the woods, Jed stopped so abruptly that Bubba almost ran into him. "This as good a place as any," he said. "Sit down." Bubba sat on a fallen log, his heart pounding. "Understand there been some hard words 'tween you and Israel."

Bubba just stared at the carpet of pine needles.

"Now let me tell you something onct and for all," Jed spoke cold and firm. "I done put up with you treatin' me like you ain't got no respect, but there's one thing I ain't gone stand for, and that's you talkin' like that to a man what's been your friend and a help to us all. Ain't no call, and I won't have it."

"Didn't think you wanted us to be beholden to them no more," he muttered.

"Man brings us seed corn, and that man my friend, you'd best believe I'm gone be beholden. Everybody needs help sometimes, and we need help now, or we lose this farm. You want that?" He shook his head, his spit turning sour. "I didn't think so," Jed nodded. "Son, only thing worse than needin' help yourself is havin' a friend needs help what won't let you help 'em. Pride can be a good thing, but we're supposed to be humble, too. That's why the Lord gives us trouble and friends, so we can learn nobody lives alone on this earth."

"Israel ain't no friend to us."

His father blinked. "What you say?"

"Nothin'." He looked away.

Jed's eyes stretched wide. "You say Israel ain't no friend? Ain't he the man helped you out while I was gone, taught you how to hunt and fish and farm? You don't call that friend?"

"Friend don't hurt you behind your back."

"Israel ain't done nothin' to you."

"Didn't say to me, said to you."

"You know somethin' I don't, spit it out."

Cornered, Bubba gave way. "Israel's the one ran that still. He's the one let you go to jail."

"How you know that?"

"Saw him at the still the day I got lost. He was sittin' on an old tree stump and cryin'. Then he took a piece of wood and wrecked that place to bits."

"He see you?"

Bubba shook his head. "I was hidin' in the weeds. He picked up that old drum and threw it, just threw it right across the clearin'."

"That don't tell you it was his still."

"Saw a piece of pipe." Bubba looked away. "Saw it onct before when I was little, over to Israel's. Hadn't never seen a pipe like that, a pretty copper color, coiled around like a piece of rope." His voice dropped. "Saw that same pipe at the still. Israel was crushin' it around in his hands. Threw it, too."

Jed's shoulders sagged, and he let out a long breath. "I thought so. I thought so," he said.

"You knew?" Bubba's voice cracked. His last hope had been his daddy would tell him he was wrong.

"No, I didn't know," he shook his head. "Just a feelin'. Too much seemed to add up that way."

"Then why . . ."

Jed held up his hand for silence and walked to the edge of the clearing to think, then turned back to face Bubba. "I know your question, and you got a right to ask. I just don't know if I can answer so you'll understand. You see, Israel was my friend."

Bubba's eyes widened. "He ask you to go to jail?"

Jed shook his head. "We never talked about it. He never said the still was his, and I never said I thought it was. We go back a long ways, son," he went on, "and there's some things don't need to be said 'tween friends. I gave Israel his right to keep silent, and he took it. But I trusted him enough to know he wont gone keep silent without a mighty good reason. And that was good enough for me."

"So he just let you go to jail."

He shook his head hard at Bubba's bitter tone. "Wont like that. We was all caught 'tween a rock and a hard place." He leaned forward, as if willing Bubba to understand. "What you think would have happened if Israel had admitted he was the one runnin' that still?"

"He'd have gone to jail instead of you."

"Ain't so simple. One thing for a white man to make a little 'shine. All he gets is jail and people turnin' their backs. But you know good as I do, what goes for a white don't necessarily go for a colored."

"But folks wouldn't have thought so hard of Israel. Folks like him."

"Yes, most do. But he's still colored. You got to remember it was hard times then. Folks were dirt poor, and nerves was on edge." Jed looked at him straight, "Israel would've been a dead man, son. He'd already had one run-in with the Klan. They find out he makin' 'shine, that would've been all the excuse they needed."

"But you didn't know for sure it was him."

"It wont a chance I could take, knowin' he might be killed. And his farm would be gone, and what would have happened to Lily, and her bout crazy with grief already over Benjamin?"

Bubba hadn't thought about that. "Whyfor Israel want to run an old still in the first place?"

"Ain't no tellin', but I got my thoughts. That land

he's got was passed down from his daddy's daddy, and that's all he had, just that little piece of land and a son to leave it to. And no money comin' in, and taxes comin' due, and you know how that goes . . ."

Bubba nodded, remembering the tenants in the wagon on the road that wet winter's day.

"I figure Israel must've got caught in a bind and tried to make himself some money the only other way he could see how. To this day, I don't believe he knew he was puttin' that still on my land 'stead of his."

"But you left us all alone. We could have lost our place, too."

Jed's eyes were sad. "Tell you true, I never thought they'd find me guilty. I had me a good name, and I thought folks knew I wouldn't run a still. But I was wrong, and then all I could do was hold on till I could get home again. At least I knew Israel would help look after you and your mama."

"And you and him ain't never talked about it?" Jed shook his head. "Then how you know? How you know he didn't just run that old still, make him lots of money, and let you take the blame?"

" 'Cause I know Israel. Ain't no friend truer."

"Seems to me he ought be beholden to you then, 'stead of us to him."

"Told you, beholden got nothin' to do with friendship. What I did for Israel, I did freely. He would've done the same for me." Bubba tightened his lips, and when he didn't answer, Jed's voice hardened. "If you

213

can't see your way clear to that just now, you'll have to take my word for it. But for now I got to make it clear I won't stand for no sassin' him. He's comin' over in a while, and I want you to act decent." Bubba didn't raise his eyes. "You hear what I say? You gone walk up to Israel like a man and tell him you sorry for what you said. You in the wrong this time, son, pride or no pride."

Bubba stood up, but he still wouldn't look at his father. None of it made any sense to him. He didn't understand grownups at all. That's the way they were, he didn't want to be one. The way he saw it, Israel owed the apology to them.

24

The last two weeks hadn't been too bad, Bubba thought. He and Israel had acted civil, and so the work got done. He hadn't apologized that day like Jed wanted him to — just spoke. And Israel had said "Mornin'," but he hadn't joked around like he used to.

This morning the woods stood with their tops in a mist of new green, and spears of sunlight slanted down as he walked in the soft April air with a string of catfish swinging from his hand. He was glad he'd checked his trotline early. His mama would be pleased, for there was enough fish for supper and to sell. He came out into the sunlight and climbed the hill. Standing among the tombstones, he saw below the gray wood of the homeplace softened by the spring green of the chinaberry tree and the yellow arching branches of his mama's forsythia bush. He felt a satisfaction at the new-planted fields, for soon they, too, would be fuzzed over with green, this time with rows of beans and corn instead of weeds.

And there had been company to make the days pass quicker. Of course Lily visited regular, but other neighborhood women came, too, since Scooter'd been hurt. Those times, Lily would quietly fold up her sewing and leave. Ruby had been torn, but she finally had to accept Lily's quiet decision. They both knew the ladies weren't likely to stay if a colored lady was there, too. It made Bubba mad at first, but now he was glad to see his mama laughing and talking with the ladies like she used to.

Even Mrs. Fields had come in her fancy Lincoln to tell them the school board had decided to fire Ole Raggey. "We decided his fault finally outweighed his good, Ruby," she'd said. Bubba had stared, wondering what the good had been and not liking her calling his mama Ruby when his mama called her Mrs. Fields.

"What's Ole Raggey gone do now?" Bubba had asked his mama that night. "You reckon he'll move away?"

"Not likely. This here's home, and he's got enough land to make a living. Money wont the satisfaction he got out of teachin'." She looked at Scooter rocking in her chair with his cast resting on the arm and sighed. "He wont always like he is now, you know. My mama said he was the nicest boy you'd ever want to meet." Bubba had a hard time imagining that. "Then when he came back from the war, he was different. When he first started teachin', all the girls had a crush on him."

Bubba looked amazed. "On Ole Raggey?"

"He wont old then, son. He was a war hero and right nice-lookin'. Considered quite a catch, he was."

"Did you like him?"

She shook her head. "Oh, I had my chances, but there wont never anybody for me but your daddy."

"You mean Ole Raggey liked *you?*" Scooter put in.

"Well, you don't have to say it like that!"

"He didn't mean anything bad, Mama," Bubba said. "I bet you were the prettiest girl in school."

"Go on with you," she laughed. "Anyway, seems like he didn't know how to quit fightin'. Things went wrong, he blamed everybody but himself. Couldn't get what he wanted, had to be somebody else's fault." Bubba wondered if what Raggey'd wanted had been his mama. He never had got married, and maybe that was why. "He's sure one miserable man," she went on. "I tell you boys, hate and spite are worse than the typhoid. They'll burn you up from the inside out. Man's got to give and forgive, like the Good Book

216

says. Else the main person he harms is himself." Bubba had shivered like a cold hand had touched him on his neck.

Now he shivered again in spite of the warm sun, thinking how Ole Raggey might have married his mama if it hadn't been for Jed. And now he'd lost his job, and people were turnin' their backs, so that hate for Jed Harkins would likely be burnin' harder.

Israel's truck passed on the road. Out of habit, Bubba waved, but Israel kept looking straight ahead. He let his arm drop back to his side. He hadn't meant to wave anyhow. Shifting his string of fish to his other hand, he headed home.

The next Saturday, seemed everybody was coming to visit, first Doc Swinson and now Mr. Tetley.

As soon as the doctor's car had pulled in, his daddy had headed for the house, leaving Bubba alone in the field with Israel. "Seems like Doc done pick today to get that cast off Scooter," Israel said. Then as another car turned in, "Hmph, look like Mist Tetley goin' a mite fast." Bubba held the mule steady as he looked back at the homeplace in time to see Tetley rush into the house.

"You think you can get this mule home by yourself, boy?" Israel asked. He nodded, and as Israel hurried away down the row, Bubba remembered the last time Mr. Tetley had come unexpected. He slapped the reins, praying the mule wouldn't turn stubborn. He didn't have a speck of water with him to pour in its ear to get it going.

As he got nearer, he saw the men clustered on the porch. Mr. Tetley seemed to be doing all the talking, and nobody was smiling. Then he and Jed shook hands, Swinson jammed his hat on his head, and they left.

Bubba hurried from the barn in time to hear his father say, "I got no notice. Wasn't expectin' this."

"Been 'spectin' somepin'," Israel said. Bubba came up to the porch, but they paid him no mind.

"You think Raggey can get away with it?"

"He got powerful friends. Sheriff's one of 'em. 'Sides, this here farm worth havin'," Israel added.

Bubba's spit dried up. What's Ole Raggey got to do with our farm?

"Well, he's not gone get it," Jed snapped.

"Then he got to be stopped," Israel said. He added softly, "You know what I got you got."

"Let me think about it."

"Best not wait too long."

"Can't do nothin' till Monday anyway. I got to think." Jed brushed off his pants and walked toward the back field, his hands tucked in the bib of his overalls.

"Ole Raggey after our land?" Bubba asked.

"Not my place to say." Israel's eyes were veiled.

"My daddy wouldn't never get rid of this farm."

" 'Spect not," Israel nodded. "His family done held on to this place so long it a part of hisself."

"Then ain't nothin' to worry bout. He don't sell, Ole Raggey don't get."

Israel glanced after Jed's retreating figure. "They's other ways, for them what don't care how they comes by somepin'."

Bubba's chin came up. "Huh. He don't scare me."

"Boy, you got more hair than you got sense. Snake'll bite just as hard whether you scared or not." He put his hand on Bubba's shoulder, "But don't you go worryin' none. Things gone work out fine." Bubba pulled back — he wasn't a little kid — and Israel dropped his arm. "Reckon I best be gettin' home. Your daddy needs me, he knows where I'm at."

Bubba watched him go, then climbed up into the chinaberry tree to still his jumbled thoughts. It whispered like an old friend as a stray breeze fluttered the new leaves. This was his family's place. His daddy would never sell. Didn't he just say Raggey wont gone get it? Then he remembered Israel saying the sheriff was Raggey's friend, and Bubba knew.

Taxes. They owed and hadn't paid. If Raggey said something in the right ear, the county would come, ready to foreclose. A sheriff's sale, and no mule to sell to raise money this time. Bubba licked his lips and looked around. He tried to picture them gone and their homeplace empty, or worse, somebody else living there.

219

He saw Israel's figure vanish into the woods. Ole Israel hadn't been gone six years. He'd had all that time to harvest good crops and put aside plenty of money to pay his taxes, he thought bitterly. And then he realized that they might be beholden again, because his daddy might have to borrow from Israel, borrow money that by rights would be theirs anyway, if his daddy'd been home to work their farm and Israel had gone to jail instead.

Now who was beholden to who? His thoughts whirled, and his chest felt tight, like he was wrapped round and round with a rope and couldn't breathe. Like they were all bound up together and couldn't move without the other, and they'd never get free. And the rope was of Ole Raggey's making, and he was holding the end, just laughin'.

25

Ruby had loaded up the table with enough Sunday dinner for three families. She always took her worry out on cooking, like food would cure anything, Bubba thought as he pushed at the broken pieces of pie on his plate. He wasn't the only one not hungry. Almost none of the food had been touched.

After Israel had left the day before, Jed had walked around like his mind was afar off, till even Scooter gave up asking questions. His mama's eyes had looked strained, and even the puppy sensed something was wrong. It had slept resting its head on Jed's foot, and he hadn't even noticed. And through his window that night, Bubba had heard his mama's porch rocker creaking and her soft voice as she prayed.

This morning at church hadn't been much better. Folks had cut their eyes away from his daddy and Ole Raggey both and talked serious among themselves. Then afterwards, the crowd had broken up quick, except for Shade Fields and Mr. Tetley coming over to speak. His father's head stayed high, and his mama kept a smile on her face, even if it didn't look like a natural one. When they'd gone to church at Easter, folks had thought they'd known about their land being sold up, but they hadn't. It made a difference, now they knew. Now they all acted like the Harkinses were already gone.

Well, we ain't. There's still tomorrow, Bubba thought. Surely his father would find a way to keep their place without borrowin' money from Israel. He speared a bite of pie, but his stomach rose to meet it, and he put it back down.

Israel's truck rattled into the yard. Ruby put down the plate she'd been scraping, and a look passed between her and Jed. Through the screen door, Bubba saw Lily getting out of the truck, and he was glad. His mama needed a friend right now. Jed went out, and he and Israel walked off across the yard. Bubba nodded to Lily, then slipped out to follow them. I got a right to know what's going on, he told himself. And he wont gone eavesdrop.

He found the two men sitting on the bench by the barn, chickens pecking at the dirt at their feet. Jed only nodded as Bubba came near. Israel's eyebrows rose, but then he also inclined his head. Bubba sat cross-legged on the ground, not wanting to call any more attention to himself. He might get told to leave.

Israel said, "What I got ain't good news. I been askin' around. Somebody seen the notice in Allton. Said it wont the county foreclosin'."

"Not the county?" Jed looked surprised.

"Somebody been buying up the tax sale certificates these last three years."

Jed let out a soundless whistle. "And now they want their money."

"Or this land."

Bubba's stomach went into a knot, and his worried eyes looked from one man to the other as Jed said, "Anybody know who holds them certificates?" Israel shook his head. "You reckon Raggey's in on this?"

"Ain't no tellin'. Don't doubt he'll be at the sale, though. Too good a chance to get you back."

"Gone cost more now. Interest to pay, too."

"That's right." After a moment, Israel said, "You decided what you gone do?"

"Not yet."

"Got to do somethin'. Waitin' time is up," Israel said. Jed rubbed his thumb on his palm. The big man leaned forward. "Somebody gone bid on that land tomorrow. For sure Raggey gone be one. You willin' to take that chance?"

Jed shook his head. "Too big a chance to take."

Bubba's breath came out in a relieved sigh.

"All right," Israel said, "we got that settled. When you want to go?"

"Israel, I don't want to take . . ."

"Look, this ain't no time for pride," Israel said. "You in a corner. Best back out anyways you can." His voice dropped. "You done for me, and I knows it. Ain't nothin' I could ever do pay you back enough."

"You don't owe me anything."

"Ain't a question of owe," Israel shook his head. "You my friend, I your friend. Ain't fittin' you holp me and not let me holp back."

They're talking about the still, Bubba thought.

"Been many a time you done for me."

"And many a time you been there for me. You want to start keepin' score?" Israel's voice rose.

Bubba had never seen him flare so. And his father looked like he was digging in stubborn, too.

"I didn't say that," Jed said, abrupt.

"Sound like it to me." Israel got up and walked a few steps away, then stood with his back to them. Jed kept working his thumb on his hand.

The silence was so tight Bubba heard his blood humming. He hated to borrow from Israel, too, but they might lose their land if they didn't. Hadn't Israel said eatin' pride was a dry feast? And wouldn't Raggey be more than a mite pleased to get their homeplace?

An edge of red caught his eye — the handkerchief he'd given Israel for Christmas was sticking out of his back pocket. He remembered how proud he'd been then to get something he knew Israel would like. Like a movie show, the memories came back — Israel on their Christmases, pleased and laughing at him and Scooter opening their presents, his patient hands showing how to put a worm on a hook, and his proud look when Bubba did something right. He remembered how when he was little he'd pulled out his grandaddy's old gun and asked Israel to teach him how to hunt, and how the blamed thing had gone off. No harm was done, 'cept to his feelings, but Israel had turned it all around so Bubba'd thought he'd done somethin' special. It wasn't till a long time after that he realized he hadn't really shot the man in the moon and left a new scar there.

He looked again at the man standing there with his hands hanging loose, bowed down with wanting to help any way he could, just like he always had, and Bubba realized he hadn't been putting on an act all those years. He was just Israel, true to the bone, loving him and Scooter both. He felt his hurt slide away and fought back a yearning to touch him. Bad enough to have done somethin' wrong, but here he was trying to make it right, and Jed Harkins wouldn't let him. He'd been wrong about Israel, but his father was wrong, too, not to let him help. He could almost see the wall between the two men. Daggone grownups, what they have to fight for now anyway? Actin' like they didn't have good sense. A wash of temper pushed Bubba to his feet. He took a deep breath and said, "Huh!"

He got their attention. Israel turned around just as Jed looked up. Bubba shifted to stand square on both feet and spoke his mind. "Seems to me you two diggin' yourselves in a hole. You want to fight, that's fine with me, but the time come we lose this place, you gone do the explainin' to Mama about who done what to who and how many times, and maybe that'll make it easier for her." He blinked at sudden angry tears and headed for the house, ears strained to the silence behind him.

Finally Israel spoke. "Boy is right."

" 'Spect he is," Jed said.

"You gone listen to reason?"

Bubba stopped, not wanting to get out of earshot.

"Looks like I got no choice."

"Good, got that squared away."

"I'll pay you back soon's I can," Jed said.

"Just be payin' your ownself. Yours much as mine."

When his father didn't answer, Bubba's heart sank. He could feel the wall going up again. Israel must have felt it, too, for he sighed. "Cross that bridge when we get to it then."

"We'll see," Jed replied.

Bubba peeked back and saw the two solemnly shake hands. Then Israel cuffed Jed on the shoulder. "Got to get my mess movin' then. You get yourself ready, and I be back to get you soon's I can. Best we go to Allton tonight, then we be there first thing."

"Sale don't start till noon."

The big man nodded, "And we be already there." He grinned, "Ole Raggey ain't gone win this time."

Jed grinned back. "For sure not."

"We fix him."

"Right and tight."

Smiles wide, they shook hands again. As he passed Bubba, Israel said, "Boy, you got a big mouth, but for one time you put it in the right place. Obliged." Bubba didn't know what to say, so he only smiled. Israel winked back. "No time to waste now," he called back to Jed. "You be ready when I gets back. Don't want that man to get a head start on us."

"I'll be ready," Jed said, and then Israel was gunning the truck out of the yard. He turned to face Bubba. "I'm leaving it up to you to take care of things while I'm gone."

Bubba took a deep breath. "I want to go, too."

"Ain't no need."

"I got a right."

"You got a responsibility. Somebody needs to stay here to look after your mama and do the chores."

Bubba looked away. Finally he nodded.

"Ain't no need to be so long-faced," Jed went on. "Israel and me, we'll do our best to save this place."

The silence stretched out, then Bubba felt Jed's hand on his arm. "Glad you changed your mind bout Israel. Don't want to take no money off'n him, but needs must, and he won't take no for an answer."

"He got a right, too," Bubba said under his breath.

Jed inclined his head and walked back to the house.

Bubba let his tension go and uncrossed his fingers. Ain't no way I'll stay, he thought. This my place much as his. Six years ought to count for somethin'. He looked at the chinaberry tree, waiting and still against the darkening sky.

26

The clock struck nine as Israel's truck pulled up. From upstairs, Bubba heard his parents go outside.

He had come on up with Scooter, saying he was tired. His mama had raised her eyebrows but not said anything. Scooter hadn't even noticed Bubba was dawdling, he'd been so worn out. He looked across at his brother sprawled out on the bed, sound asleep. Wont any holding him down since he'd gotten that cast off, Bubba thought. Last night he'd favored that arm, but he was up at first light, playing. In the silence at dinner, he'd quieted down, his eyes going from his mama's face to his daddy's, but once free of the house, he was laughing again, rolling his hoop on the lane.

The boy turned over, muttering in his sleep. Scoot ain't gone grow up no place but here, Bubba vowed, ignoring the doubt that clung like flypaper. Shoving something deep in his pocket, he went downstairs.

He slipped out the back into the cool night, making his way to the front in the shadows. In the light from the windows, he saw Israel leaning against the truck fender and his daddy with his hands on his mama's shoulders. They weren't looking his way. He sprinted quietly across the ground, pulled himself up over the tailgate, and dropped into the truck. He crouched down and held his breath, sure they could hear the loud beat of his heart, but they kept on talking, their voices soft against the night. The bare boards and metal strips of the truck bed felt cold as he lay down out of sight, the lump in his pocket pressing into his leg.

"We'll be back by late tomorrow," his father was saying. "Don't you worry yourself into a fret now. Everything's gone be all right."

His mama's voice was quiet. "I know it will. The good Lord ain't brought us this far to let us down now."

Then there was nothing but silence. After a moment, Israel asked, "You bout ready?"

"Guess so," Jed said. "Thought sure Bubba'd be here to see us off."

"No tellin' where he's at," Israel said.

"He went on to bed," Ruby answered.

"This early?" Israel sounded so surprised Bubba had to muffle his laugh. "He takin' sick?"

"Prob'ly poutin'," Jed said. "He didn't like it too well when I told him he couldn't come."

" 'Spect not. He as bound up in this place as you."

The truck dipped as Israel got in. Bubba put his head down tight on the truck floor when Jed opened his door. He waited, his muscles tight, praying the dark in the corner was dark enough. Then Israel revved up the engine, and the next thing he knew, the truck bed slammed against his chest as they hit the deep pothole at the foot of the lane. Bubba didn't dare raise up, so he squirmed around to brace himself against the side rail. Now he wasn't jarred so much, just felt the grinding vibration. The night air flowed cold down the truck sides, and his hair blew in the wind. His ears started to hurt, and he hugged himself for warmth. And they were going all the way to Allton.

The two quick blares from the horn startled him, making his heart drop, until he realized they were passing Lily's, and it was Israel's "goodbye."

When they stopped at the crossroads, Bubba spotted something bulky on the other side and took a chance. Careful to keep his head down, he stretched, and his hand grabbed something soft. It unwound, and quickly he rolled himself up in the folds of the quilt, pulling the corner end up over his head. As he warmed, he smiled. He bet Israel had put that quilt in the truck for him. Prob'ly figured his daddy would have somethin' to say about Bubba goin' with them, and that something would be No. His smile widened. Israel knew I wont about to stay home. He snuggled down into the warm and let the truck sing him to sleep.

Lights flashing red against his eyelids woke him and blinded him into a squint. Upside down, the street-lights looked funny, like one moon passing by after another. Then the truck entered a tunnel of trees, and Bubba could only see a dark canopy of branches and leaves overhead. He knew it wouldn't be long before the truck stopped and his daddy and Israel found him. He started working up an excuse.

The smell of popcorn made his mouth water as the top of a movie theater marquee went by, the light circling around. He raised up to see more, but the truck swerved, and he had to reach out to keep from falling. Suddenly they screeched to a stop, knocking him against the back of the cab. The doors slammed and there the men stood, one on each side, as he struggled to get free of the tangling quilt.

"Well now, lookahere. Looks like we picked us up somethin' along the road," Israel teased, grinning.

Bubba swallowed the dry lump in his throat and pulled harder at the quilt.

But his father didn't think it was funny. "What you doin' here, boy? Thought I told you to stay home and look after your mama." Bubba didn't know what to say. "You hear me? I'm waitin' for an answer."

"Curiosity got the best of him, I 'spect."

"Wont that," Bubba said quickly. Jed's eyebrows went up. "I got to know if we gone lose our place."

"You find that out soon enough when we got home."

"Not soon enough for me."

Jed looked at Israel. "I swear, kids are the world's worst for turnin' up where they don't belong."

Bubba flared. "I ain't no kid. I got me a right to know what's goin' on. I took care of that place for six years, and it's my homeplace, too. I got a right," he repeated, his jaw set.

"Boy's got a point there," Israel said.

Holding his breath, Bubba waited for his father's answer. He gripped the lump in his pocket.

Jed rubbed the back of his neck. "Mayhap you're right." He looked at Bubba. "But let's get this one thing straight. You stick right with us, no runnin' off, no puttin' your mouth in. You here to watch and that's all. You understand?"

Bubba nodded, glad to breathe again. He saw Israel's secret wink and felt better.

"Well, I sure am glad to hear that wont no haint I

saw raising up that quilt in that back window," Israel laughed. "Thought maybe that bear of Bubba's done left the woods and jumped right in this here truck." Bubba wished Israel would forget that dumb bear.

A smile pulled at Jed's mouth. "Thought you were gone lay me up on that windshield, you stopped so fast."

"You see somepin' like that, you stop fast, too," Israel said. "Hey Bubba, you reckon you can unwrop yourself while I find us a place to park for the night? Didn't bring that quilt along just for you, you know." Chuckling, he got back in the cab. Jed looked at him with a strange expression, but when Israel started up the engine, he shrugged and got in, too. Bubba busied himself with the quilt while they drove through the quiet residential streets.

When the truck stopped again, Bubba realized they were deep into colored town. A few lights shone from the windows of the weathered houses, and syrup cans full of sprouting flowers lined the sagging porches, reminding Bubba of Lily's red geraniums. As the two men got out, he headed for the tailgate to climb out. "No point doin' that, boy," Israel said. "You can holp me spread these covers so we can get us some sleep." He looked at Jed. "Figure this be safe as anywhere. You don't mind?"

Jed shook his head. "Hand me that quilt, Bubba," he said, pointing to the other end of the truck bed. For the first time, Bubba realized there was another quilt rolled up, with a couple of Lily's best pillows shoved up behind it. He felt let down that Israel hadn't brought the quilt for him after all, until he remembered that secret wink. Grinning, he scrambled to the corner and unrolled the new quilt, and handed the end to his father.

Later, he snuggled down between the two men, remembering suddenly the nights he had spent with Benjamin when he'd been little. He puzzled at the memory until he realized it was the smell of the quilt taking him back. Lily always threw a handful of herbs in her wash water, and her things always had a peppery sweet smell that made him want to sneeze. He hadn't remembered that since Benjamin died. The ache of missing his friend swelled stronger than it had in a long time. He turned over again.

"Boy, you gone make your nest all night?" Israel's voice came soft.

"Can't seem to get to sleep."

"That teach you to sleep on the way. Though how you managed in this rattly truck on that rough road is beyond me."

Bubba giggled. "Wont so hard, once I got warm."

"Reckon you was glad I brought these here quilts."

He grinned into the dark and could feel Israel smiling, too. Jed turned over, muttering in his sleep.

Bubba held himself as still as he could. The whisper came again. "You wake him up, you gone get whatfor. Close your eyes now. He needs his sleep, and you need yourn. Tomorrow a big day." Then he turned over, too, and Bubba found himself wedged between their two backs, but he didn't mind. It felt good.

Soon Israel's breath settled into a soft snore. Bubba stared up at the stars glittering in the lacework of branches above him and realized it was a chinaberry tree. He wished himself home. He was scared.

What if Israel ain't got enough money to outbid Ole Raggey? A picture rose in his mind of tenants on their place — somebody else working the fields, another towheaded child there, his hair lifting in the breeze as he swung on the branches of the chaineyball tree, some skinny slack-jawed woman working in his mama's kitchen, all because one man had more money than another. It wont right. Ole Raggey'd fair be struttin' in his pride that he'd finally got back at Jed Harkins.

He dast not close his eyes now, he'd have nightmares for sure. Bad enough that time he'd dreamed they was on that wagon and that creature behind. It had taken him a long time to get shut of the feeling that dream had left.

And now it had all come down to this: two men and a boy asleepin' in a truck, waitin' for day to come, and not knowin' what it would bring, for good or bad. Rubbing the lump in his pocket for reassurance, he stared out into the dark, the air drying his eyes till he blinked again and again, fighting off sleep for fear the dreams would come and they would be worse than what was real.

27

Bubba saw the sun come up. In the dim morning, he heard the soft cooing of a pair of turtledoves and then sometimes a raised voice or laughter as people stirred in their houses. Down the street, a door slammed and someone whistled "Oh My Darlin' Clementine." A robin echoed the song from the chinaberry tree. The sight of the branch swaying under the bird's light weight sent a wash of homesickness over him. The tree's purple and white flowers were just coming into bloom, their light lilac fragrance perfuming the air. He decided to take it as a sign that things would be all right.

He couldn't lie there another minute; his skin was crawling from staying still. He glanced over and found Israel looking at him. "Mornin', Squirmtail," he said.

Now Jed stretched, and Bubba sat up with relief. "Who you callin' squirmtail?" he said. "I been just as still as I could get. A body got to turn over sometimes. No way to sleep with you two gruntin' and snorin'."

Israel chuckled. "Reckon he told us off that time." He sniffed the air. "Mmm, mmm, don't that bacon smell good? Feel like I could eat a horse."

"I'd be satisfied with just one of Lily's biscuits, long as I had some coffee to go with it," Jed said.

"Well, we ain't gone get nothin' just layin' here." He poked Bubba. "Get out of my way, boy, and let me at the steering wheel, and we see what we can find."

Bubba jumped up and pulled the quilts out of Israel's way as he clambered out of the truck.

Israel had parked beside the road after first pulling up at a rickety store to get them coffee. Bubba and his father had waited in the truck while he went in. The colored men on the weathered gray porch avoided their eyes and stayed impassive and silent the whole time Israel was inside.

Back on the road, Israel had pulled off to the side. Now Bubba sat cross-legged between the two men, savoring the warm spring sun. A field of tobacco stretched out behind them, the new plants green specks against the gray dirt.

Jed reached for another ham biscuit. "Nice of Lily to pack us some biscuits."

"She know better than to send us off without none." Israel looked at Bubba, who had his mouth full. "Know this here boy, too. That's how come that jar of pear preserves got in there." Jed stopped chewing.

Israel grinned. "Tell you the truth, figured that boy be comin' along, you tell him no or not."

His father didn't smile back. "Expected him to do what I said."

Israel looked straight at him. "He done what you said for six years, but he got a mind of his own."

Bubba looked from one to the other.

" 'Pears like you know him better than I do."

"Just been around him more," Israel said, and then the laugh lines around his eyes crinkled up. "He just like you — he don't want to miss nothin' neither."

Jed studied his coffee, then a smile tugged at his lips. "You sayin' the pot's callin' the kettle black?"

"You said it. I didn't."

"Truth's truth, I reckon." He took a deep swallow, then looked at Bubba. "But that don't mean you can get away with it regular, you hear?" Bubba nodded and took another bite of his biscuit. Jed looked up at the sun, " 'Fore God, I'll be glad when this day is over."

"Mr. Tetley say that sale gone start at noon?"

"Noon sharp, on the courthouse steps."

The biscuit went dry in Bubba's mouth. Israel brushed off his pants and stood. "Reckon we'd best get on back then. Won't hurt to be there a mite early. Might be able to find out some more."

Jed nodded and poured the rest of his coffee on the ground. He stood aside for Bubba to get in the cab first. Bubba was glad because he sure didn't feel like riding alone in the back. Seemed like that biscuit had lodged solid before it got all the way down. He breathed deep to loosen the tightness in his chest.

The corridors of the county courthouse stretched out long and gleaming as their steps echoed on the hard floor. The smell of disinfectant and stale cigarette smoke hung in the air. Jed looked down at Bubba as they approached the tax office. "I meant what I said, now. Too much at stake this day to have things go wrong because of some boy." Bubba opened his mouth, but Jed cut him off. "You behave, or you can wait in the truck. That clear?"

"He be all right," Israel said.

"Just don't want nothin' to go wrong," Jed repeated. He had put on his suit in the men's room and now made a final effort to smooth the wrinkles from the flimsy fabric, then gave up. "You all wait right here. I won't be long," he said.

They slid onto the smooth bench. Bubba burned with resentment, his fear forgotten.

"Don't let it eat at you, Bubba," Israel said. "He got a lot on his mind."

"I ain't no little kid," he said, his jaw tight.

· "For sure not," Israel grinned. "Best way to prove that is act it. That tell him somepin'."

Bubba's attention was caught by the people going by with spit-shiny shoes and important airs. A

238

woman passed, her hair waved in sharp curves, and he wrinkled his nose at her perfume. He itched to move. "All right if I walk around a minute?" he asked.

"Ants in your pants?" Israel asked. "Don't go too far. Your daddy gone be out soon."

Bubba took his time walking down the hall, his hands in his pockets. At the open courthouse door, he saw some posted papers flapping in the breeze and walked over. He held the fluttering page still with his hand. It had his daddy's name on it in uneven type, with a long paragraph about their farm and then the date of the sale and where. He looked at it for a long time, then went back inside.

As he turned the corner, he saw Oscar Raggenbotham coming down the hall. The man glanced toward Israel, but went by without speaking. Then Jed stepped out of the office and came face to face with him. Jed looked at Raggenbotham with a hard eye, then turned his back and walked over to Israel.

Whew, he must be some mad. Bubba hurried over.

"Ain't no more than we thought," Israel was saying.

"Sorry underhanded trick," Jed snapped.

"You 'spectin' somepin' else?" Israel's eyebrows raised up. "We knew he out to get you somehow."

"But he's been settin' this up these past three years! Plannin' it!"

"Man ain't no fool," Israel said, shaking his head. "He know a good place to put his money."

239

"You know as good as me it wont just the money."

Bubba couldn't keep quiet any longer. "What's wrong? What's Ole Raggey done now?"

Jed's eyes looked blank with rage. "He the one done bought up those tax certificates on our land."

Bubba's skin prickled. "You mean he got our place?"

Jed shook his head, grim. "Not yet, he ain't. He just holds them certificates, and now he got himself a writ of foreclosure. That's how come sale's been called." He looked at Israel, his eyes worried. "Ain't no way in heaven we got enough money to outbid that man, he makes up his mind to have my farm."

"Mayhap he just want his money out of them certificates and ain't interested in your place."

"You believe that?"

The silence stretched out, Bubba holding his breath. Finally Israel shook his head. "No." Jed's shoulders sagged, and Bubba let go his breath, too.

The courthouse clock started chiming. Jed looked at them. "Well, might as well see it through. Let's get on outside." Israel opened his mouth, then shut it. Jed asked, "What you were gone say?"

"Just hopin' Miss Ruby's prayers can pull a miracle this time."

Jed stood quiet. Then he said with a new firmness, "Well, the good Lord's gone 'spect us to do our part. Maybe we're givin' up too soon."

As Jed headed for the door, Bubba felt a flash of

pride at his straight back and head held high. That's the way his daddy had used to look, the way he'd looked the day he'd left to come to this same courthouse and been sent away to jail. Any justice in this world, Bubba thought, Ole Raggey ain't gone get away with this. He put his chin up and straightened his back, too, as he followed his father out to the courthouse steps.

28

A quiet crowd had gathered on the lawn in front of the courthouse, shifting and murmuring like a field of tall corn under a hot summer wind. Squinting against the sudden brightness of sun-white concrete, Bubba looked around at the somber faces and didn't see a single soul he knew. A shackly wagon filled with worn household goods and a thin cow tied behind was parked on the street. A dried-out man held the mule's reins, and a woman waited in the wagon, her poke bonnet pulled forward, her hands slack. Two ragtailed children played unheeding on the strip of grass beside the sidewalk.

As he followed his father and Israel down the steps and they moved into the group, Bubba kept his eyes on his father's back, the heavy smell of sweat and the dark mood of the people pressing at him so he felt the need for air. Israel tried to stay toward the back, but Jed took him by the arm and led them to an open spot up close enough to see. Once they broke free, the first thing Bubba saw was Raggey standing over to one side, looking straight at Jed. He was smilin' the same way he used to when he would give a whippin'. Bubba looked up at his father. "You see Ole Raggey over there?"

Jed nodded but kept his eyes straight ahead.

"He's smilin'," Bubba said.

"Let him smile. Mayhap it won't be for long," Israel answered.

Please, Lord, Bubba thought.

A child's laugh pealed out, and people turned their heads to see. One of the tenant children was somersaulting on the grass. The man slapped the little girl across the ear, the sharp crack loud in the silence. A thin wail keened into the air as the handprint came up red on the child's white cheek. "Hush that," came the woman's voice, flat and unmoved.

"What they doin' here?" Bubba asked Israel.

"Somebody done called them due, too."

"But tenants don't have no land."

"They signed a note on what they got — furnishin's, animals, goods."

"They ain't gone have nothin' left?"

"Likely not," Israel said. "They ain't the first been sold up, nor the last."

Bubba looked over again. The child had gone back to her playing. The woman still sat in the wagon, her shoulders humped, and the man rubbed the mule's neck as he talked to it. Bubba's heart turned in his chest. Maybe there wont no justice after all.

The gathering stirred as some men came out on the steps. One dressed in a light brown suit stepped up and arranged a stack of papers on the wooden stand.

"Who's that?" Bubba whispered.

"Lowrimore, commissioner of the court," a voice in back of him answered. He turned around, and there stood Mr. Tetley. Bubba was glad to see him, but then he saw Tom Sly behind him. What you reckon he come to Allton for? Bubba wondered. He gone bid too?

"You find out anything new?" Tetley asked Jed.

"Just who been buying up them certificates."

Tetley's eyes followed his toward Raggenbotham. "Can't say I'm really surprised," he said. Bubba felt let down. He acted like it was nothin'.

"Well, took me back a bit, I tell you," Jed said. "Hard to think of a man planning his revenge that far back. Three years a long time."

Tetley paused, then said, "You ever think it could go back farther than that?"

Bubba could tell his daddy hadn't from the expression on his face. "What you mean?" Jed said.

"I mean, he's been hating you a long time, from what I hear. Doesn't seem likely he would have waited until three years ago to start planning something."

Israel pursed his lips and nodded. "That's right. Man wants to get back at somebody, he wants to get 'em then."

"People say somebody turned in the information on that still," Tetley said. Bubba's neck was getting a crick, but he didn't want to take his eyes off the men.

"You think he wanted me sent off to jail?"

"Could be something to consider," Tetley nodded.

"The man may hate me, but he'd know I wouldn't have nothin' to do with no still."

"Wouldn't matter," Tom Sly said. Bubba looked around so quickly, his neck caught. "Man's land hungry anyway," Sly went on, an edge to his voice. "He found out about a still on your land, don't matter to him if it's yourn or not. He'd get a chance to get the land just the same, what with you off at prison and all."

"I doubt he would even care whose still it was, if it fell in with his plans," Tetley agreed. "A man doesn't stop to ask questions when he pulls an ace out of the pack. He just counts himself lucky and plays the ace."

Jed and Israel looked at each other. Israel said, "Fits too good, don't it, not to be true?"

Jed looked down at Bubba. "Reckon if your mama hadn't had the good sense to sell that mule, he would've had our place before this."

"He ain't got it yet," Israel said, his lips firm.

"You got that right," said Tom Sly. "He come to the wrong county this time."

His mind busy trying to absorb what he'd heard, Bubba hardly noticed the crowd's murmurs or when the lawyer at the top of the steps said his daddy's name and droned on into a description of their land. He was remembering Ole Raggey with that smirky smile when he'd ask how him and his mama was doing, and then his sour look when Bubba told him about selling the mule to pay taxes. And the way he looked at his mama when she wasn't noticing. The cutting remarks he'd made about prisons and niggers and the Harkinses.

Israel was right — it all fit together too good. 'Cept he bet Raggey *had* known who was running that still, that he'd had them caught both ways. If his daddy had told on Israel, Raggey still could've got Israel's land, and that would have hurt his daddy just about as bad. When Jed had kept his mouth shut and gone to prison in Israel's stead, Ole Raggey had prob'ly been grinnin' from ear to ear.

And here he was smilin' again, like a cat about to jump. Well, they weren't whipped yet. Bubba fingered the money sock in his pocket. He'd brought it along just in case Israel and his father didn't have enough. After all, it was his homeplace, too. Then the reality weighed on him again. Might not even be a drop in the bucket now they knew who held the notes.

Somebody bumped him. He turned and looked

straight into Mrs. Fields's face. Her cheeks had pink spots, and she had on her best Sunday dress. And Shade Fields stood beside her.

Then he saw more people behind them: Mr. Charles, and Doc Swinson, and Henry Howell beside Ray Foster, even Preacher Satterthwaite. They all come to see their land sold up? They hate his daddy that bad? He wanted to shout out Ole Raggey was the one they should ought to be turning their backs on, 'stead of Jed Harkins.

But then he saw Mrs. Fields smiling at him, and Tom Sly's hand resting on his daddy's shoulder, and the way people had formed a semicircle like a shield around them. Bubba wondered if they had heard Mr. Tetley talking. He suddenly remembered the teacher that day with Shade Fields outside the church. Maybe this wont the first time he had told his suspicions. Folks must have known somethin' to come all this way.

He looked over at Raggey standing alone with his feet slightly apart and his hands folded together in front of him, just waitin'. He looked just like them army men in the newsreels, Bubba thought, 'cept he didn't have a gun standing on end in his hands.

He don't need no gun. He got a weapon just as bad in them papers the lawyer's holding. He remembered the men at the store talking once about holding off a sheriff's sale with guns, and he wished they had some guns with them now.

Lowrimore's voice changed its tone, and the crowd rustled. Bubba felt their resentment pushing against his back as the lawyer called in a loud voice, "What am I bid for this fine piece of property?"

Quiet hung in the air. Jed's jaw clenched. Bubba figured he was waiting for somebody else to open the bids, then he'd try to match it. The silence strung out till Bubba felt ready to jump out of his skin; his heart was hammering like a rock knocking around. Far off he heard a dog yipping, but here even the birds were hushed, like they were waiting, too. Why didn't somebody say somethin'? Ole Raggey standin' there like he ain't got a worry in the world, and just a smilin'. And me with only a dollar in my pocket. One dollar.

The crowd laughed, shattering the silence like glass. Startled, Bubba looked around to see what was so funny, but instead found everybody looking at him. Heat traveled up his neck to his face when he realized he must have spoken out loud. He didn't dare look at his father for fear he was angry — or even worse, laughing, too. Everybody else was, even the lawyer.

"Now young man, you know that land is worth more than that. You too young to bid anyhow," Lowrimore said, his smile not reaching his eyes. "You just let us grownups take care of this."

Bubba felt the crowd move like a force behind him. Jed's voice was low. "Give me that dollar, boy."

His heart dropped. His father looked mad as could be, his face set and his eyes unyielding. He held out his hand. Bubba pulled the sock out of his pocket and almost dropped it as he pulled out his silver dollar.

The crowd whispered as Jed tossed the shining coin in his hand, his eyes turning their fury on Raggey, then Lowrimore. Bubba felt like a fool, but at least he knew now his father's hard look wasn't for him. He felt Israel's hand on his shoulder as Jed turned to the lawyer waiting on the courthouse steps.

29

Jed Harkins threw his head back. "I ain't too young," he said. "I'll bid this here boy's dollar."

Bubba heard the crowd take in its breath.

Lowrimore shifted and glanced over at Raggey before he said, "You're old enough to know that land can't be sold for a dollar. It's worth more than that."

"Worth a lot more. You can't set no price be too high for what that land's worth to me." Jed squared his shoulders and spread his feet apart. "Can't put no price on a man's home. A dollar worth just as much as ten thousand to that man." The crowd muttered, then quieted again as he stepped forward. "I bid this here dollar. You gone take my bid or not?" Bubba watched his straight back and felt his throat closing up. Please, Lord, don't let them laugh again.

But nobody did. Flustered, Lowrimore kept looking Raggenbotham's way. Bubba glanced over and saw that Doc Swinson and Mr. Charles had come up beside Raggey. Swinson said something and Raggenbotham's face flushed, even though he kept looking straight ahead. Then he moved as if about to bid, but Charles stepped in front of him.

"Seems to me this man has put in a bid, Lowrimore." Shade Fields's voice came clear and firm. "And seems like no one else is goin' to. I suggest you knock it down." Bubba turned and saw Mrs. Fields look at her husband in surprise, then shut her mouth and nod.

The people around Bubba nodded, too, and started murmuring among themselves, the buzz rising like a swarm of angry bees. And Ole Raggey still didn't say anything. Bubba kept waiting for him to bid, but he only stood there, his hands clenched tight at his sides, Swinson and Charles grim-faced beside him.

Preacher Satterthwaite called, "He's right, Lowrimore. We haven't got all day."

"Knock it down!" Ray Foster yelled, and other voices joined him, a lot of folks they didn't even know. Seemed to Bubba like a lot of pent-up feelings came out, for they shouted with a will. Lowrimore glanced back at the two men standing behind him.

One raised his eyebrows, but the other nodded. Lowrimore looked again at the impassive Raggenbotham, then sighed and hit the gavel on the stand. "One dollar once, one dollar twice. Last call for bids, and it's gone."

Bubba held his breath. No one spoke. Lowrimore's face turned red, then the gavel came up again, and Bubba saw the sweat stains under his arm. The gavel hung in midair, then Lowrimore slammed it down, "Sold for one dollar to the man in the gray suit."

The crowd burst into a yell and pushed forward to slap Jed on the back. Bubba stood apart, letting it all sink in. Then he saw Israel laughing as he and Jed shook hands, and he realized it was all over. They'd got their land back. He blinked, and blinked again. He saw his father coming toward him in a haze, but he could tell he was smiling. He stopped a distance away. The people around them quieted as the man and boy looked at each other. Jed's grin widened. "We did it, boy!"

Bubba nodded. His throat had closed up.

"Ain't you got nothin' to say?" Jed reached up to brush back the hair that had fallen across his forehead.

Bubba's heart started hammering. He'd seen that gesture before, long ago. "No sir," he whispered. The familiar blue eyes held steady on his.

"Well then, you got too big to give your daddy a

hug?" Jed asked, "or are you still my boy?" He opened his arms, and Bubba saw the calluses on his hands. He suddenly recalled the carved wooden figure of the boy he had been, and he knew his daddy had waited long days just like he had for him to come home. A flutter of excitement went up into his throat. He took a step, then broke into a run and flung himself into the waiting arms.

Then people were slapping them both on their backs, but he buried his head in his daddy's shoulder, for the tears were coming. He heard Jed whisper, "Come on, son, this is a happy time," but when he looked up, his daddy's eyes were wet, too.

Before he knew it, he was up in the air, for his daddy and Israel had made a seat with their arms to lift him so everyone could see. The crowd cheered, and he even saw Mrs. Fields dabbing at her face with one of her fancy lace handkerchiefs. They led a parade of people across the grass toward the courthouse steps.

As they approached Raggey, his daddy and Israel set Bubba down gently. A hush fell on the crowd behind him as Jed and Raggenbotham came face to face. The familiar feeling of dread washed over Bubba. Ole Raggey's face showed no expression, but a muscle twitched at the corner of his eye. Bubba waited, but his daddy didn't speak, just exchanged a long look with the man. As the silence drew out, a red flush inched its way up Raggey's neck. Finally, Jed broke the quiet in a soft, cold voice, "Best you should stay away from me and mine from now on, Raggenbotham. You done enough harm."

Raggey's head came back, like a snake about to strike, Bubba thought. "Harm? I'd think you'd be grateful. Hadn't been for me, your place would have sold for taxes long ago. You ought to be thanking me," he said with a sly smile. "But I guess that's too much to expect of prison bait."

Jed's eyes narrowed. "I'd be careful what I say, were I you. Some might wonder who to call worse, an innocent man sent to prison, or the man sent him there." Raggey's eyes flicked from Israel to Jed. He tried to speak, but Jed forestalled him. "Seems to me there's worse crimes than runnin' a still, like beatin' children and buyin' poor folks' land when they're caught short. Thievin' under the law is thievin' all the same."

Fury wiped across Raggey's face, and his arm came up to strike. Time stretched as Bubba saw his arm lift, the signet ring flash, and the pulled-back shirt cuff reveal the mark on his arm. He wanted to move fast to protect his daddy — his mind told him Raggey was moving fast — but it was all so slow, and he couldn't seem to move. Then Israel's hand grabbed that arm, brown against white, stopping it, bending it back. Bubba felt the crowd freeze, and gulped. No matter what happened or how good a friend, no colored man touched a white.

"Get your hand off me, nigger!"

But Israel pulled the shirt sleeve farther back, popping the cuff open to show a welted, twisted scar. Raggey snatched his arm back. Israel stepped closer, his eyes almost narrowed shut. "It were you all the time. It were you killed my boy."

Bubba caught his breath. Benjamin?

No one moved as Israel's accusing voice carried across the shocked crowd. "I seen you that night. I seen that scar. When you raised your hand to throw that burning torch, that white robe fell back, and that scar burned in my brain, just like you burned my boy."

Now Raggenbotham looked scared as Israel's big body dwarfed his. For every step Israel took forward, he took a step back. "Your boy wouldn't be dead if Jed Harkins hadn't interfered," he blurted.

"You crazy as a loon." Israel hit the words with contempt. "He ain't to blame for what you done. His the hand that throwed that fire? His the hate?" Raggey's eyes flicked away. "Nobody killed my Benjamin but you, but you afraid to face that." Israel went on, still relentless, "You hide by passin' the blame like you hide in that white robe, but ain't no hidin' from yourself. You know and I know and God knows, and God ain't mocked." He took another step, and Raggenbotham almost stumbled as he moved quickly back. Israel put his face right up next to his. "You always got your eyes on other peoples 'cause you look in the mirror at yourself, you blush for shame."

Raggenbotham's face drained of color. He looked at

the crowd, but people shifted their eyes away. Bubba felt a fierce pleasure at seeing Raggey treated as his daddy had been.

But now Israel, hovering like the Judgment, had backed Raggey some distance from the onlookers. Uneasy, Bubba looked around. Others seemed as disturbed as he was. Tom Sly studied the ground like he could find some answers there, Mrs. Fields had her handkerchief wadded up to her mouth, and the preacher was shaking his head. A low mutter started through the crowd, but nobody moved to take Raggenbotham's part or stand by his side. Bubba looked at his daddy, but Jed's eyes were on Israel. A warning hand touched Bubba's arm, and he looked up into Shade Fields's worried eyes.

Raggey jerked his sleeve back down over the scar. The tic fluttered under his eye as Israel stepped forward again, but this time Raggey stood his ground. His bitter voice carried across the grassy space to the crowd, "You'll be sorry for this day, Israel Wade. I'm not the only one doesn't want your kind around here."

His words didn't faze Israel. "Say what you means. Ain't no nigger gone own no land, nor have him a decent life. You gone kill him and his children, and all for a piece of dirt you ain't gone work and love no way." He sneered, "Big, tough soldier man, hidin' in his mama's white sheets."

The onlookers pulled in their breaths. A ruffle of fear raised the hairs on Bubba's neck. Israel's fury had brought flecks of spit to the corners of his mouth, and his eyes were wide. Bubba realized he wasn't even seeing Raggey anymore, he was so mad. Jed tensed to move, but Fields caught his arm. In a panic, Bubba ran past them and grabbed Israel's back pocket, red handkerchief and all. "Israel!"

The big man stopped and looked down at Bubba, a puzzled expression on his face. His eyes were like a stranger's eyes. "Israel, don't!" Bubba said, and saw the man's eyes wet with tears, and he hurt for Israel's old pain opened up new. "It won't do no good, just like me beatin' Grady didn't do no good."

"He killed my boy."

"He good as kill you, too, you let him make you be like him, all eat up with hate." Now he had Israel's attention, Bubba kept talking, knowing it sounded like babble but not caring so long as he kept him safe. From the corner of his eye, he saw Raggey inching away. "That's what Lily said," he went on. "She said the man what killed Benjamin was burnin' in his own hell, and best to leave him there. Better than bein' in your own hell."

The man let out a long sigh, and his eyes looked like Israel's eyes again.

Bubba caught a glimpse of Shade Fields's relieved face and the crowd drifting away. He put his hand on Israel's arm and spoke softer. "You go to jail, you leave Lily alone, and ain't nobody can save you this time."

Israel jerked, his eyes wide. "You knows?" Bubba

255

nodded. " 'Fore God, Bubba, I never meant your daddy to go to jail for me."

"I know that now. He done it of his own free will." Their eyes locked, and he stated flat, "And I ain't gone let you go to jail neither." Then he grinned, "Lily wouldn't never give me no more biscuits."

Israel blinked. "Boy, for the work you done this day, Lily gone make you all the biscuits you want." He looked at Raggenbotham's retreating back. "You right, he ain't worth my hatin'. He one pitiful man."

Bubba slipped his hand in Israel's, and they walked back together to join Jed.

30

Once his daddy had the deed secure in his pocket, they headed home, a line of cars and trucks following behind. Tom Sly had about worn out the horn on his truck as they'd pulled away, and others had taken up the chorus, till Bubba guessed the people in Allton were glad to see the last of them head out of town.

Wedged between the two men as the truck kept up a steady vibration on the road, Bubba wanted nothing more than to see the lane for home, the house and the chaineyball tree, and his mama and Scooter. His stomach rumbled, but he knew his mama would have a feast ready. She'd prob'ly been cooking all day, workin' out her worry and hopin' for the best. And she'd be ready to celebrate, for hadn't the last thing she'd said to his daddy been, "The good Lord won't let us down now"?

And He hadn't neither.

As Israel whistled under his breath, Bubba suddenly felt lighthearted and joined in, singing "Oh When the Saints Go Marchin' In." When his daddy and Israel started singing with him, it felt like the truck rocked with their music down the highway. They sang their way home past farm fields of new growth and tobacco barns with advertisements painted on their sides and people sitting in ladder-back chairs, out enjoying the sun in front of crossroads stores. The three drawled out words to make each other laugh, even made up words and hummed when they couldn't think of any, until they finally gave out of breath. Israel slapped Bubba on the knee, saying, "Ain't this boy some smart? He ain't careful, he gone grow up to be a songwritin' somebody. Be on the *Grand Ole Opry*, I bet."

But Bubba didn't think so. He recognized some of the landmarks now, and then they passed the Fosters' house. He looked back just in time to see Ray Foster turn off from the parade, tooting his horn and waving.

Bubba shook his head. "For sure I ain't goin' nowhere. Our farm is good enough for me. Ain't nothin' ever gone get me off." He shook his head again, hard.

Jed put his arm around him. "For sure not. That's *our* land, and that's where you belong." He looked at Israel. "By all that's right, he's earned it this day."

"Best dollar he'll ever spend, I 'spect."

It wont but a piddly dollar, but his daddy was right. Couldn't put a price on somebody's homeplace. He wont never gone forget his daddy spinning his silver dollar on that wood counter and telling the clerk, "This boy just bought hisself a piece of land with his own money," and how she had smiled. Bubba had halfway expected his father to pull out one of his own dollars, but he hadn't. He'd told Israel that Bubba's was the dollar he bid with and Bubba's was the dollar bought it and Bubba's was the dollar gone pay for it. He'd felt then like his heart would burst.

He smiled again as his eyes soaked in the familiar countryside. He leaned forward. Benjamin's graveyard, then the Wades' house. Israel tapped the horn, and Lily came out on the porch as they drove by. She waved and lit out running across the yard, her flowered dress flashing purple and white as she disappeared into the trees. Then they passed the hill, and Scooter waiting there. When he saw them, he started jumping, and the puppy ran in circles.

A horn behind them blew exuberantly as they turned in, three quick taps and a long one. Bubba looked back, startled. The Lincoln whooshed on by, but not before he'd seen Mrs. Fields with her mouth gaped open in astonishment at Mr. Fields, her lace collar fluttering in the wind from the open window.

Now he could see the house, and Scooter was running down the hill, Sheba tumbling behind, ears flapping. As the truck headed down the lane, his mama came out on the porch, shaded her eyes against the glare, then came running, too, her red dress bright in the sun. And all the while Israel was blowing his horn like he couldn't hold himself in any longer.

As soon as Ruby got near, he slammed on the brakes, for Jed was fumbling with the door. He scrambled out, and Ruby was in his arms, her dress hiked up when she reached for his neck, and he swung her around like she was a girl and he was just a boy. And here came Scooter, running full tilt, then stopping short, till Jed let Ruby loose. Bubba watched from the window of the truck as Scooter took off again, leaving puffs of dust behind his flashing heels, and jumped into his daddy's waiting arms.

Israel looked down at him. "Pretty sight, ain't it, boy?" Bubba nodded. "Ain't you gone get out? You been squirmin' all the way home."

"In a minute." His eyes were memorizing the house, the barn, the smokehouse, and the chinaberry tree loaded down with blooms, it seemed overnight. Swallowing, he tried to get the words past the lump in his throat. "Want to thank you for what you done, offerin'

259

your money and all. And all the help you been. I guess I acted pretty bad there for a while, and I'm sorry."

Israel looked at him steady. "You ain't got nothin' to be sorry for. And what I done ain't nothin' to what all your daddy's done for me."

Bubba nodded, then he grinned. "You want to start keepin' score?"

Israel let out a shout of laughter and leaned across him to push open the door. "Get outta here, boy. Go give your mama a hug."

Bubba climbed down. Sheba was waiting, her tail rotating her rear end. Then Scooter grabbed him around the waist, saying, "We thought you all was never ever comin' back, and it's been the longest day I ever saw, and I been helpin' Mama, and she fixed a cake and I got to lick the bowl!"

And then his mama came over, tears standing in her eyes. "Ain't it wonderful, Bubba? Ain't the Lord good to us all?" She pulled him into her arms, patting his back as she hugged him. "Your daddy told me what you done, and I'm that proud," she whispered. Sniffing, she flicked her fingers under her lashes and laughed. "Bout time you all got home. Thought you were never comin'."

"Good thing they did," Lily said, "else you would have cooked up enough to feed everybody from here to Allton." She smiled at Israel, "She been in that kitchen all day."

Jed laughed. "She just about had 'em all to feed.

Seemed like everybody around here went to Allton with us." Ruby's eyebrows went up as her mouth rounded into an O. "We'll tell you all about it later," he said. "Got a lot of good news to tell, ain't we, son?" Bubba grinned back at his daddy. "I bet you ain't got so much food we can't lay a hurtin' on it," Jed continued. "You lookin' at three hungry men. Wont for your biscuits, Lily, we would have starved to death."

"And them preserves," Bubba added.

She laughed and gave him a playful rub on the head. He ducked back.

"We gone have company for dinner," Ruby announced, but she was looking at Bubba, "so you all best wash up good, else you won't get nothin' to eat."

Company? What was his mama talking about? And why was she staring at him like that? He looked down at his hands. They didn't look that dirty to him.

She sighed. "Boy, I do believe you ain't got the eyes God give you."

"He ain't noticed a thing," Israel chuckled.

Jed gave Bubba a push. "Don't you reckon it's about time you spoke to that pretty thing awaitin' up there on the porch? She looks a mite lonesome to me."

As Bubba stumbled forward, he saw Thora standing in front of the door, her hands folded in front of her. She had her Easter Sunday dress on, and her red hair caught the light. Suddenly his feet felt like lead.

"Go on," Israel said. "She ain't gone bite."

"Hush up, Israel Wade," Lily said. "He just shy."

"She's been waitin' with me all day, Bubba," his mama said softly, smiling. "I sure been glad of her company."

"I like her," Scooter said. "She's almost as good as a boy. She can climb trees better'n you can."

Then Bubba saw that her knees were skinned and a rip gaped in the hem of her dress. Suddenly she was just Thora again, and his feet would move. As he passed under the chinaberry tree, the perfume from the flowers filled his nose, like it was saying welcome home, and he smiled. And Thora smiled back.

$$\frac{99}{1} \quad \frac{60}{11} \; ()$$